THE DEATH OF FRIENDS

THE DEATH OF FRIENDS

MICHAEL NAVA

G. P. PUTNAM'S SONS
NEW YORK

G. P. Putnam's Sons
Publishers Since 1838
200 Madison Avenue
New York, NY 10016

Library of Congress Cataloging-in-Publication Data

Nava, Michael.
The death of friends / by Michael Nava.
p.   cm.
ISBN 0-399-13977-X
I. Title.
PS3564.A8746D43   1996   95-26308   CIP
813'.54—dc20

Printed in the United States of America

1   3   5   7   9   10   8   6   4   2

This book is printed on acid-free paper. ∞

Book design by Brian Mulligan

FOR KATHERINE V. FORREST

The death of friends, or death
Of every brilliant eye
That made a catch in the breath—
Seem but the clouds in the sky
When the horizon fades;
Or a bird's sleepy cry
Among the deepening shades.

W. B. Yeats
The Tower

Jesus said, "If you bring forth what is inside you, what you bring forth will save you. If you don't bring forth what is inside you, what you don't bring forth will destroy you."

The Gospel of Thomas

THE DEATH OF FRIENDS

1

I WOKE TO FIND THE BED SHAKING. SOMEWHERE IN THE HOUSE, glass came crashing down, and on the street car alarms went off and dogs wailed. The bed lurched back and forth like a raft in the squall. The floorboards seemed to rise like a wave beneath it, and for one surreal second, I thought I heard the earth roar, before I recognized the noise as the pounding of my heart. My stomach churned and fear banished every thought except *get out.* And then it stopped, the bed slamming to the ground, a glass falling in another room. Outside, the car alarms still shrilled, the dogs whimpered and the frantic voices of my neighbors called out to another, "Are you okay? Are you okay?" I sat up against the headboard and drew deep breaths. My heart beat slowly returned to normal, and I became aware that someone else was in the room. I reached for the lamp, but the power was out.

"Who's there?" I called out.

My eyes accustomed themselves to the darkness, but I could not see anyone among the familiar shapes of the room. Yet I was sure someone was there, hovering at the foot of the bed, watching me. It moved, and then a great wash of emotion passed over me. Sadness. Relief. Regret. I felt them but they were not my feelings. I reached out my hand, but there was nothing. The room began to rattle, shaken by an aftershock. It lasted only a few seconds and when it was over, I was alone again.

I hopped out of bed and ran into the closet door. The blow stunned, then focused me. "Think," I commanded myself. Clothes. Shoes. Flashlight. Get outside. I pulled on some clothes and headed for the kitchen for the flashlight. The usual hum of appliances was stilled. Glass crunched beneath my feet as I crossed the room to the small pantry, where I found the flashlight in a utility drawer. I shot a beam of light across the kitchen. The cupboards had swung open, cans and boxes spilling out of them. The refrigerator had been knocked a couple of feet from the wall. I was suddenly very thirsty, and I opened the refrigerator to find its contents spilled and shaken. I drank some orange juice out of the carton and thought of Josh, alone in his apartment. I picked up the phone but, as I'd expected, the line was dead. I got out of the house.

The street where I lived ran along the east rim of a small canyon in the hills above old Hollywood. On maps of the city, it was a curving line off Bronson Canyon Drive, hard to find and seldom traveled. My house, like other houses on the block, dated back to the 30s, but, unlike them, possessed no particular architectural distinction. It was down a few steps from the street, behind a low hedge, the bland stucco wall revealing little of the life that went on there.

I'd bought the house when I'd moved to Los Angeles from San Francisco seven years ago and I'd lived there with my lover, Josh Mandel. Now I lived alone, Josh having left me thirteen months earlier for another man who, like Josh, had AIDS. It was Josh's belief that, because of this, Steven could understand him in ways that were inaccessible to someone like me who was uninfected. But then Steven died and Josh's own health began to deteriorate. I would gladly have taken him back but he insisted on living on his own. Still, we'd had something of a reconciliation, drawn back together by memories of our shared life and the impending end of his.

As I closed the door behind me, I considered driving to West Hollywood to check up on him, but I doubted whether I would get that far. The quake had undoubtedly knocked out traffic signals and the roads would be filled with panicked motorists and nervous cops. I remembered the spooky presence in my bedroom and wondered anxiously if it had been Josh, but that was absurd. It had been nothing more than a trauma-induced hallucination; a momentary projection of my terror.

I went around the side of the house and turned off the gas. When I returned to the street, my next-door neighbor, Jim Kwan, approached me, flashlight in hand, and asked, "Hey, Henry, you okay?"

"So far," I said. "Of course the night's still young. How about you?"

"We came through in one piece. Knock on wood," he said, rapping his forehead. "I'm going to check on Mrs. Byrne down the street."

"I'll come with you," I said, anxious to keep busy.

We passed a group of our neighbors huddled around a radio. The radio voice was saying, ". . . is estimated to be a six-point-six quake centered in the San Fernando Valley, with the epicenter near Encino . . ." I was relieved to hear that because it meant Josh was at least as far away from the epicenter as we were and there didn't seem to be any major damage to the hill.

I heard the clatter of metal against the street and trained my light on Kwan's feet. He was wearing cleated golf shoes.

"What's with the shoes, Jim?"

An embarrassed smile crossed his round, good-natured face. "I was scared shitless, man. I grabbed the first shoes I could find."

I shone the light on my own scuffed Nikes and recognized them as a pair Josh had left behind.

"Is your phone out?" I asked Kwan.

"Look across the canyon," he said. "Everything is out."

Through a gap between two fences I could see the west rim of the canyon, where far grander houses than ours commanded breathtaking views. Darkness. The October night was beautiful, cool and mild. Without the distracting blaze of city lights, the stars glittered in the deep blue sky. A damp herbal smell came up from the undergrowth. I reached down, tore a sprig of rosemary from a bush and crushed it between my fingers. The scent calmed me.

"Spooky, huh?" Kwan said. "Like the city was clubbed in its sleep."

"Did you feel anything strange in your house after the quake?"

"Like what?"

"I'm not sure," I said. "Like a ghost?"

Kwan laughed. "Something must've come down on your head, Rios."

I felt the bump on my forehead where I'd hit the closet door. "Maybe so. Maybe I just imagined it."

Mrs. Byrne was sitting on her porch steps reading her Bible by candle-light. She was an old woman, her mottled, veiny face framed by stiff white tufts of hair. She had lived in Los Angeles for over forty years, but still pronounced the name of the city with a hard Midwestern "g." Once or twice a month she went door to door with a sheaf of religious tracts of the hell-and-brimstone variety, and raved at the neighbors polite enough to let her in about God, Satan, kikes, spics, niggers and chinks. I barred the door when I saw her coming but Kwan, whom she usually caught while he was out gardening, suffered her rants with good humor. When I kidded him about it, he said she was lonely. With good reason, I replied.

"Mrs. Byrne, are you okay?" Kwan asked.

She looked at him with rheumy eyes and said, "Didn't I tell you, Kwan, it's the last days. Earthquakes, fires, plague." Her voice got high and a little crazy. "Jesus is coming."

"Just in case he doesn't come tonight, I'm going to shut off your gas," he said. "Keep an eye on her, Henry."

She squinted at me. "Who are you?"

"Your neighbor from down the block," I said. "Henry Rios." I sat down beside her and asked, "The quake scare you, Mrs. Byrne?"

"Knocked me clean out of my bed," she replied. "But I've been through worse, and worse is coming, young man." She rattled her Bible. "Now you take this AIDS—"

I trained my light on her Bible and said, "Why don't you read to me until Kwan gets back?"

She opened the book and began reading in her high, shaky old woman's voice. As I listened, I felt the kind of euphoria people feel when they survive a disaster. I realized then that I'd thought I was going to die in the quake. My mind drifted back to that moment after the quake ended when I'd imagined there was someone else in the room. Was it just a hallucination? It—whatever it was—had seemed so real. Then Kwan came back and put an end to my ruminations.

For the rest of the night, I huddled with my neighbors around the radio, listening to reports of the damage. Most of the city was dark and there were reports of fires, leveled buildings and downed freeways, but the worst of the damage was confined to the valley. To my relief, damage to West Hollywood was reported as minimal. For a while, the echo of sirens reverberated on the hill from the streets below, but by dawn it had quieted down. As the sky began to lighten, our little disaster party broke up and we trudged back to our houses.

A boy was sitting at my front door, asleep. I came down the steps and I stood above him. Occasionally, homeless people wandered up the hill, but he was too clean and well-dressed for that. His arms were wrapped around his knees and his head was down, long, black hair covering his face. I had no idea who he was, but I was pretty sure he hadn't stumbled into my doorway by accident. I'm a criminal defense lawyer and accustomed to strangers showing up at my door at odd hours of the day and night.

I didn't particularly welcome these unexpected visitations; I'd always seemed to attract a class of clients who were, as a disgruntled ex-partner once put, "from hunger, Henry." I was a magnet for the desperate, frightened and reviled, who somehow or other had heard about the fag lawyer who was a sap for a sad story and let you pay on installment. Josh used to tell me, "You're a lawyer, not a social worker," but I didn't take his point until after he'd moved out, leaving me with plenty of time to wonder if he would've stayed had I spent less time on my clients' troubles and more on ours. So I'd taken a sabbatical from the law to ponder that, and other mysteries of my midlife. I'd gone into therapy like a good Californian, and learned that in all probability the reason I'd devoted myself to the legal lepers of the world was because I felt like an outcast myself—"queer," in every sense of the world—and I struggled to compensate with good works.

In the end I'd taken this insight and decided, so what. I was forty-two years old, and law was all I knew or cared about, apart from Josh and a few friends. I'd resumed my practice on a very small scale, handling mostly appeals and working out of my house. Occasionally, a fellow defense lawyer would refer me a particularly hopeless case. I wondered which one I had to thank for the sleeping boy.

I hunched down on my heels, shook his shoulders gently and said, "Wake up, son." He raised his head and his eyes fluttered open. They were unusually blue, which was surprising, given his dark coloring. I judged him to be in his mid-twenties and he was strikingly handsome: long hair, dark skin, blue eyes and a silver loop in either ear. Wearily, he got to his feet. He was short, no more than five-seven or -eight, but tightly muscled, a featherweight. Beneath loose-fitting jeans and a black pullover sweater, his slender body radiated tension and fatigue.

"Are you Henry Rios?" he asked nervously.

"Yes. Who are you?"

"Zack Bowen," he said. "I'm . . . Chris Chandler's boyfriend. Can I talk to you?"

For a moment, I was too astonished to answer. Chris Chandler's boyfriend?

"Come inside," I said.

As soon as I stepped into the house, exhaustion hit me. I'd been running on adrenaline since the quake and it was all used up. I left Zack Bowen in the living room and went into the kitchen to figure out some way of making coffee that didn't require either electricity or gas. There was still some hot water in the tap, so I mixed two cups of muddy instant and carried them into the living room. Zack was stretched out on the couch, asleep again. I sipped the vile brew and thought, Chris Chandler's boyfriend. Well, well.

2

CHRISTOPHER CHANDLER WAS A SUPERIOR COURT JUDGE WHOM I'd known for twenty years, since we'd been law students together at Stanford in the mid-'70s. He was married and his wife, Bay, had also been a friend of mine back then. They had a son, Joey, and they lived in Pasadena in a beautiful house on an elegant street. Chris was generally agreed to be a comer, smart, fair and ambitious—and straight. It didn't hurt that his father-in-law, Joseph Kimball, was the senior partner at one of the city's biggest and most politically well-connected law firms. Chris was thought to be a shoo-in for elevation to the federal bench next time a Republican occupied the White House. That had always been his goal, even when we were students, and the most casual review of his judicial career revealed a certain amount of calculation in that direction. Nothing too damning, a provident change of party affiliation, a reputation as a tough sentencer in criminal cases, that sort of thing.

Any hint of excess ambition on his part was leavened by his and Bay's indisputable commitment to good works. She took the lead there, serving on the boards of numerous organizations that ranged from a battered woman's shelter to an AIDS research fund. Occasionally, flipping through the *Times*, I'd come across a picture of them at a charitable event, all dressed up in tux and evening gown. "Impersonating adults," I'd tease Bay when we talked, which happened maybe two or three times a year. I crossed paths more frequently with Chris, since his courtroom was downtown where I handled the majority of my cases, but for having once been such good friends, I saw very little of them.

I know this puzzled Bay who, over the years, made many attempts to revive our student friendship. She saw through my polite evasions of her offers of dinners with the family, and when I did accept I knew she was aware of my discomfort. I tried not to show it because I genuinely cared for her. She was straightforward and good, though not without edges. Like me, she was a recovering alcoholic and prone, as most ex-addicts are, to bouts of depression and gusts of dissatisfaction. I know she was ambivalent about having become, as she once joked, "a society lady with causes." This, I reminded her, was an improvement on her mother, who had simply been a society lady, bone-thin, self-absorbed and distinctly without causes. She laughed at that. But I didn't have a glib retort when she said, "We're old friends, Henry. You know there aren't any secrets between us."

She was wrong. My friendship with her had always been based on a deception. Just like her marriage.

Chris had been a year ahead of me at Stanford, but the school was small enough so that we were on nodding terms. In my second year, we had a class together and we moved from a nodding to a speaking acquaintance. I was twenty-two years old, and when I was not in class or studying for class I could be found making timid excursions into the frenetic gay world of San Francisco in the mid-1970s. That those two parts of my life, law student and homosexual, seemed irreconcilable bothered me considerably, because I couldn't see having to choose one over the other. I had wanted to be a lawyer from the time I was a boy, inspired by biographies of Lincoln and Clarence Darrow, and Perry Mason on TV. As for the other thing, well, I hadn't exactly planned on being homosexual, but I knew I was by the time I was sixteen; knew it, and knew I could no more change it than I could change the color of my eyes. My problem was how to be homosexual and a lawyer at a time when being gay was grounds for disbarment in most states.

If there were any other gay students at the law school, they kept it to themselves. I often wished there were, if only to have had someone to talk to about my dilemma, but not for that reason alone. I was a reserved and inexperienced Mexican-Catholic boy from the central valley of California, whose idea of homosexuality was derived from Walt Whitman's romantic vision of "two boys together clinging,/One the other never leaving." In my forays to San Francisco I found a lot of boys who didn't mind clinging to me for a night or two, but forever was not in the vocabulary of the times. I thought if I could meet someone more like myself I would not have felt so continually out of place. Sometimes, in class, I'd look around the room and speculate who among my male classmates might be gay. Some seemed more likely than others, but Chris Chandler was not one of them. At twenty-three, he was a square-jawed, fair-haired boy who looked like he'd stepped out of a Brooks Brothers catalogue; the kind of WASP kid beside whom I felt very much the brown-skinned scholarship student.

One night I was at a gay bar in the city, a place called the Hide 'n Seek, feeling, as usual, out of place but hopeful, if only hormonally. There were white lights above the bar, but the rest of the room was bathed in red and blue and the muggy air smelled of cigarette smoke, aftershave and amyl nitrite, a drug that jumped the heart and smelled like old socks. Disco music blared over huge speakers mounted on walls in the corners of the room. A strobe light pulsed above the dance floor, catching the frenzy of the dancers. It always amazed me that there was never any violence in the bar despite all the men crowded together, lurching drunkenly into each other, spilling drinks and burning each other's clothes with careless cigarettes. Instead, the accidental brush of male body against male body was like the striking of matches that flared and sputtered out, desire like wisps of smoke slowly thickening the air.

I was standing at the edge of the dance floor, a little drunk and feeling a bit sorry for myself, when someone bumped into me. He said, "Sorry." I turned around and said, "That's okay," and saw it was Chris. For a moment, neither of us said anything, then Chris smiled, a slanting, embarrassed grin, and said, "You're Henry, right?"

"That's right," I said. "Henry Rios. You're Chris—"

"Chandler," he said. "You're in my Corporations class."

It was a small thing, that exchange of last names, but in that world of one-night stands and first names only, it made running into him there seem perfectly natural.

"Buy you a beer?" he asked.

"That would be great," I said.

We made our way to the bar, got the beers and found a relatively quiet spot where we could talk without shouting. As if we were sitting at the pub in the student union, Chris kept up a steady stream of chat about classes, professors, fellow students and even, I remember, the Security Exchange Act of 1935. Later, he told me he'd chosen those innocuous subjects to relax me because I seemed so unsure of myself. It worked. I loosened up, and eventually we moved to more personal matters; places of origin, families, and finally, "You're gay?" and "How long have you known?" and "I would never have guessed you."

Last call was called. Chris smiled at me and said, "How did you get up here?"

"I took the train," I said.

"Can I give you a lift back to school?"

"Sure," I said, and because I was uncertain, I didn't know how to ask whether he wanted to spend the night.

He smiled again and said, "My place is quiet and I live alone."

I woke up the next morning on a mattress on the floor of Chris's tiny apartment, which was over the carriage house—now converted to a garage—of an old stone mansion in downtown Palo Alto. It was a typical student apartment, orange crates for bookshelves, a trestle-table desk, books and records everywhere and that mattress. Chris was asleep beside me. For half the night we'd just talked, and then there'd been that moment when the next most natural thing in the world was to kiss. There was none of the awkwardness with him that I'd felt with other men; the small voice in the back of my head trying to remember the man's name or the mumbled negotiations about who would do what to whom. It had never felt so good before to be with another guy, so easy and friendly—"We two boys forever clinging . . ." Well, no, I didn't think that exactly, but what a difference it made to make love to someone I could also imagine as a friend.

I got up and went to the bathroom. When I reached for the soap to wash my hands, I heard a metal clink in the wash basin. I fished around and found a ring, a plain gold band. There was an inscription inside, *To Chris from Bay,* and a date from earlier that year. I took it with me back to the bedroom. Chris was awake. I showed him the ring and joked, "What's this, you're married?"

He took the ring from me, slipped it on his finger and said, "Not yet. Just engaged."

"Zack," I said to the sleeping boy. "Wake up."

He opened his eyes, yawned and mumbled, "Sorry, I'm really tired." He sat up and cradled his head in his hands, his long hair spilling like a veil across his face.

"It's been a long night for everyone," I said. I pushed a cup toward him and said, "Here, this isn't very good, but it'll wake you up." He sipped the coffee and made a sour face. I said, "So you're Chris's boyfriend. I didn't know he had one."

He put the cup down with a clatter, looked at me with his too-blue eyes and blurted out, "Chris is dead."

I was so tired that it occurred to me I was dreaming this conversation, and that any moment I would wake up, my head filled with the receding image of bright blue eyes and the echo of "Chris is dead." But then Zack began to sob, loudly and uncontrollably, and his body shuddered as if someone had picked him up and was shaking him, and I realized I was not dreaming.

"Stop that," I said sharply.

Zack looked at me, and whatever was in my face at the moment silenced him.

"I'm sorry," he stammered.

"What happened to Chris? Was he killed in the earthquake?"

He shook his head. "Someone killed him."

That stopped me. "What do you mean?" I said sharply. "Killed? Who killed him?"

"I don't know," he said, on the verge of tears again.

"Calm down," I said. "Okay? Take a deep breath. Now let it out. Again."

He gulped air with an almost comic intensity, but it quieted him. For a moment, we sat looking at each other. There was something about Zack Bowen that struck me as childish or, rather, childlike; an exaggeration of affect, a pop-eyed emotionality.

"Feel better?" I asked him.

He nodded.

"Now let's start over," I said. "Tell me about Chris."

He took another deep breath and said, "He was working late last night. In the courthouse? I went to talk to him, but when I got there, he was on the floor and there was blood all over the place." He rushed the words as if they had a bad taste. "I felt for a pulse but he was already cold."

"What did you do then?"

"I went home," he said. "I didn't know what else to do. My clothes were—I had to change my clothes."

"Why didn't you go to the police?"

Shamefaced, he said, "I didn't think of it."

"You didn't think of it?" I asked incredulously.

"I was afraid . . ." his voice trailed off.

"That they would arrest you for killing him?"

Now he really did get pop-eyed. "I swear I didn't do it. I would never hurt Chris."

But I wasn't inclined to let him off so easily. I said, "If you didn't kill him, why were you afraid to go to the police?"

"I know what the cops are like," he said. "The way they ask you questions, you get totally confused and pretty soon you're saying things you don't mean and the next thing you know they got you."

This had a familiar ring to it.

"You've been arrested before," I said. "What charge?"

He picked at a fingernail and mumbled, "Six-forty-seven-b."

Penal Code section 647(b): soliciting an act of prostitution. That he knew the code section meant he'd been arrested more than once. I had a sinking feeling about all of this, Chris's murder, this kid. It began to have the ring of something sordid.

"You hustled?"

"A long time ago."

"Is that how you met Chris?"

"I said it was a long time ago," he replied, his eyes daring me not to believe him.

"Okay. Tell me exactly what happened yesterday," I said. "From the moment you got up until you found Chris. And Zack, tell me the truth."

"That's what I've been telling you," he said.

3

HE LIVED IN THE VALLEY AND HE WORKED AS A WAITER AT A restaurant on Sunset Boulevard in Silver Lake. I knew the place, an upscale Mexican restaurant with a tin roof and twenty-dollar entrees frequented by gay yuppies. He and Chris had not spent the night together.

I interrupted him. "How long have you been seeing him?"

"About six, seven months," he replied.

I was full of questions about how a Superior Court judge had entangled himself with an ex-hustler, if ex is what Zack was, but the immediate issue was Chris's murder, so I saved them for later.

Still, I couldn't resist asking, "Did you know he was married?"

Zack nodded.

"How did he manage to spend nights with you?"

"He only did that since he left her," Zack said guilelessly.

"He left his wife?" I said, astonished. "When?"

"Last month?" he said. "Yeah, last month. He was staying at a hotel until he could find a place. I wanted him to move in with me, but he thought that would be too hard on his son."

And too public, I thought, but just said, "I see," remembering I'd had coffee with Chris within the past month and he hadn't said a word to me about any of this. "Okay, back to yesterday. Did you see Chris during the day?"

"No. He called me just before I went to work, and asked me to come to the court when my shift was over because he wanted to talk to me."

"About what?"

He looked away. "I don't know. He didn't say."

"But you had an idea of what he wanted, didn't you?"

He looked at me as if I was telepathic. "No," he lied. "Not really."

"You said you'd tell me the truth," I reminded him.

After a moment, he said, "I thought maybe he wanted to break up with me."

"Why did you think that? Did you have an argument?"

"No, we didn't fight," he said. "Chris didn't fight, he just got quiet, like he had something to say but he wasn't saying it. That's how he's been the last few days. It drove me crazy trying to figure out what it was."

That sounded like Chris, all right, but I knew Chris. The question was, who was Zack. Most of the hustlers I'd run into were street kids with fifteen-year-old faces and sixty-year-old souls, usually violent only in their self-loathing, but sometimes capable of turning it against their tricks. I'd been thinking that something like that had happened to Chris, but Zack didn't seem to fit the mold. I didn't sense any banked rage in him, only a victim's passivity.

"How did you feel about that?" I probed. "Were you mad when you went to see him?"

He ran his fingers through the flood of his hair in a forlorn gesture and said, "No, I was afraid."

"Afraid?"

"I didn't want to lose him," he said, helplessly.

"So you went to the courthouse to see him," I said. "What time?"

"As soon as I got off work, around eleven."

"Which courthouse?" I asked, testing his story.

"The big white one," he said, correctly. "I guess it's on First Street. You go down into the garage on Olive. That's where I parked, underneath."

"Why did you park there?"

He looked suspiciously at me, as if I'd asked a trick question. "That's where I always park when I go see Chris."

"How often have you been at the courthouse?"

He shrugged. "I don't know, exactly. I have lunch with him some-times. He likes that restaurant with the earthquake design in it. What's it called, the Epicenter?"

I had also eaten lunch with Chris there. It was, inexplicably, a favorite place of his, and the fact that Zack knew this began to make it plausible to me that he was a part of Chris's life.

"What happened after you parked in the garage?"

"I went inside."

"How?"

"There's a door from the garage that goes inside the courthouse."

"The door was unlocked at eleven o'clock at night?"

"I guess there were people still working there," he said. "Like Chris."

"Did you see anyone? Did anyone see you?"

He shook his head. "No. Chris said there're guards at night, but if anyone stopped me, to tell them I was going to see him, but I didn't see any guards."

"What did you do once you were inside the courthouse?"

"There're some stairs that go up to the big lobby where the elevators are, and from there I took the elevator to the fifth floor where Chris was."

The details were all right so far. "Okay, then what? Describe to me how you got to Chris."

"There's that door, not the one to the courtroom, but the one next to it, the one that goes to Chris's office? He said he would leave it open for me. I went in and then I was in the hallway with all the book-shelves. I walked down the hall to Chris's office and the—" his voice began to break "—the door was closed."

And then I felt it too, the thud of grief dropping like a stone on my chest, and it all became very real. My own voice shook a little when I said, "Go on, Zack."

"I can't," he said, weeping openly.

"Go on," I repeated. "Please."

He took a sharp breath. "I knocked on the door."

"You knocked?"

"I didn't just want to bust in on him," he said, almost angrily. "I knocked a couple of times, but he didn't say anything, so I go, 'Chris, it's Zack.' I waited but he still didn't say anything, so I opened the door and I went in and he was—he was on the floor, on his stomach. And it looked like the whole side of his head was just flat." He raised a hand to the right side of his head. "And there was blood everywhere and this thing was still buried in his head."

"What thing, Zack?"

He was not crying now, but remembering, his face expressionless, his eyes distant. "This thing," he repeated. "Like a marble pyramid, but small, like this." He held his hands about eight inches apart. "Just buried in his head. That was the worst part. I took it out. I turned him over. There were bubbles in the corner of his mouth, blood bubbles. I thought he was still alive, because they were popping, but he was dead."

The way he described it I could feel the fug of murder in the air. I asked, "What did you do then?"

"I wiped his mouth with my shirt," he said, "and then I got out of there."

"How? The elevator?"

He shook his head slowly, as if reluctant to leave the remembered room. "The stairs," he said, after a moment. "There're stairs that go all the way to the garage. The elevator stops in the lobby. I was afraid if I got off someone would see me."

"Why were you afraid that someone might see you?" I asked him. "Why didn't you go for help?"

"Chris was dead," he said. "I had his blood on my shirt, my hands. I was afraid they might think I'd hurt him."

As gently as I could, I asked, "And did you, Zack? Did you hurt Chris? You can tell me the truth."

His face was so raw with feeling it was hard to look at. I would not have been surprised if he'd shrieked or broken down sobbing again, but all he said was, "No. No."

"Why did you come to me, Zack?"

"I had to tell someone," he said. "Chris talked about you. He said you were his only gay friend."

"Chris never mentioned you to me."

"He was going to tell everyone," he said. "That's what he told me when he left his wife. He said he couldn't live with secrets anymore."

That was another surprise. After all these years? But then what about his career? Or was this just something he'd told Zack to keep his new lover happy . . . ?

"But it's strange he would keep you a secret from me," I said.

"You think I killed him," he said.

"I don't know what to think. I'm having trouble taking this in."

A low humming started up in the kitchen, the power coming back on.

"I'm going to make some proper coffee," I said, picking up the cups. "When I get back, we'll decide what to do. All right?"

He sagged with relief.

The kitchen was a mess and it took me a moment to remember why. The quake seemed like something that had happened a long time ago. Then I thought of Josh and automatically picked up the phone, but the line was still dead.

"Who are you calling?" Zack was standing in the doorway.

"I was checking the line," I said. "It's still dead."

"You were calling the police," he said, accusingly.

"No, I wanted to call my friend, Josh, to see if he's okay after the quake. He has AIDS," I continued, wanting to talk away the tension between us. "I'm worried about him."

"I have to go now," Zack said.

"I wasn't calling the police, Zack."

He spun on his heel and was out of the house before I knew what was happening. I ran after him, but by the time I got to the street, he was speeding off in an old wreck of a car. The license plate was too grimed to make out a number. I watched him round the curve and plunge down the hill.

"Damn," I said.

This was my dilemma: I knew that Chris lay dead in his chambers where, given the fact that the quake had shut the city down, he might not be discovered for several days. If I told the police, they would go after Zack Bowen. Zack Bowen may have killed Chris, but I was not prepared to deliver him into the hands of the LAPD. This was, in part, the knee-jerk reaction of someone who'd spent his professional life defending people from the police; I didn't trust cops and, with rare exception, I didn't like them. I knew it was a tough job being a cop and I wouldn't want it, but they gave as good as they got and most of the time got away with it. Then there was the matter of professional ethics. Even if I decided I couldn't defend Zack, my job was to refer him to someone who could, not have him arrested. I would've felt that way even if I was certain he had killed Chris, and I wasn't. Then there was my personal interest. Zack Bowen had come to me with a story that implicated my own past and I wanted to hear the rest of it before I drew any conclusions about his guilt or innocence.

So I thought about it for a while, and by the time the phones came up later that morning, I'd made up my mind. I called a high-ranking and deeply closeted police captain whom I'd known for several years through a mutual cop friend in San Francisco. Captain Closet and I had even had a half-hearted sort of affair after Josh and I had broken up, testing, unsuccessfully, the theory that opposites attract.

I reached him on the first try and gave him a bare-bones and relatively truthful account of Zack's visit, without using Zack's name.

When I finished, Captain Closet said, "Let me understand, Henry. Some guy you've never seen before shows up at your house and claims that Judge Chandler was murdered last night in his chambers, then disappears."

"Yes," I said.

"And he doesn't give you his name and you have no idea of who he is."

"That's right."

"This is total bullshit," he said.

"Maybe," I said, "but don't you think you should follow it up in the event that it isn't?"

"Don't leave your house until I call you back," he said.

An hour later, he did, and confirmed that there was a body in Chris Chandler's judicial chambers.

"Is it Chris?"

"His wife's coming down to identify the body," Captain Closet said. "What's going on here, Henry? Why did you call me instead of going through regular channels?"

"Judge Chandler was gay," I said. "Not too many knew that. I figured you'd understand."

I heard him breathing softly at the other end of the line. "You think you can feed me this line about a stranger dropping in to tell you someone's murdered a Superior Court judge, I won't give you a hard time because you know about me, is that it, Henry? Blackmail?"

"No," I said, though he was exactly right. I improvised. "What I'm doing is passing along as much information as I can without waiving the attorney-client privilege, because Chris Chandler was a friend of mine and I didn't want the janitor to find his body a week from now."

"Some friend," he said, with heavy cop-irony. "You're gonna defend the guy who killed him."

I said, "I can't tell you anything else without getting into privileged information."

"You're in a shitty racket, Henry."

"Like you're not," I replied, and having made the points we always made against each other, we hung up.

Then it hit me: Chris really was dead.

4

I WAS BACK IN LAW SCHOOL, STANDING THERE IN THAT TINY apartment. The ring glinted on Chris's finger. I felt confused and betrayed and it made me brutal.

"Does your fiancée know you're a fag?" I asked him.

His pale eyes flashed anger, but all he said was, "Do you think that's any of your business?"

We were no longer two innocents on the open road, but a couple of naked and hostile strangers. I groped around the mattress for my clothes, pulled on my jeans and said, "Thanks for whatever."

He felt the change, too, and drew the sheet to his waist. "Don't go like this," he said, quietly.

"Like what?" I said, tying my shoelace, my back turned to him.

I felt his hand on my shoulder. "You know what I mean, Henry. Like some hysterical, wounded . . . Let's not act like all the rest of them."

I shrugged his hand off. "You mean like all the other queers," I said. "Well, this may be a phase for you, but not for me."

"I didn't say I wasn't gay," he said. He sighed, almost inaudibly. "I should've stopped going to bars after I asked Bay to marry me. I knew it was a mistake."

"What are you talking about?" I asked, standing up and looking at him.

"I thought I could handle going to a bar or a bathhouse now and then, just to get some relief, but I knew that sooner or later I'd meet someone like you."

"Oh, now you think I'm going to blackmail you."

"Would you just stop," he said angrily. "That's not what I meant."

"Then what?"

"Someone—some guy—I could imagine being with."

I stood there with my shirt in my hand. "I don't understand, Chris."

"Come back to bed," he said, "and I'll explain it to you."

He threw back the sheet. There was a spray of freckles across his chest, and when he moved, the morning light caught the flicker of muscle beneath pale skin. I dropped the shirt, kicked off my shoes and tugged out of my pants, and got into bed beside him. His body was warm and hard.

"Explanations can wait," I said. I was twenty-two. Flesh still had that power over me.

"Do you love her?" I asked him later.

He tucked a pillow under his head and said, "I've spent most of my life trying not to be in love with anyone because I was afraid it would be the wrong kind of love."

"What's the wrong kind of love? This?"

"It's so easy when you both want the same thing, isn't it," he said, touching my hair. "I want this, but there are things I want, too. A family, a career, to make a difference in the world. Those things aren't possible between two guys."

"You don't know that."

"How many happy couples did you see at the bar last night?"

"About as many as you'd see at a straight singles bar," I said, a little heatedly. "That's not what those places are for."

"There aren't any other places for us," he said. "That's not the life I want."

I turned to him. "We can create a different kind of life. We can make new places."

A faint, indulgent smile creased his lips. "You do those things, Henry. I think you can. But it's not for me."

"Why?"

"Listen, I'll tell you, but don't get mad, okay?"

"I'm listening."

"This," he said, squeezing my thigh, "this is about sex. I'm not knocking sex, it's great, but that's all it is, Henry. I can't organize my life around it. It's a kind of self-indulgence. You said you wouldn't get mad."

"I did not." I was mad, but I couldn't stay mad because I'd had this same conversation with myself. "How can you marry a woman if you're not being honest with her about who you are?"

"It depends on what you mean by honest," he said. "Should I tell her about the other girls I've had sex with? What would be the purpose of that? It's the same principle with the guys I've been with."

"You've gone out with other women?"

"Haven't you dated women?"

"No," I said. "It seemed dishonest. The way I define it, anyway."

"I guess I don't have your high standards," he said coolly. "I was president of my fraternity at college and there was a lot of pressure to date. I did what I had to."

"That sounds like fun."

"Come off it," he said, annoyed. "I went to a little college in the middle of Iowa. There was no way I was gonna come out."

"I had you pegged as an Ivy Leaguer."

"My family broke up when I was ten and it was just me and my mom. I was lucky to be able to afford any kind of college. I'm a scholarship student here, Henry, just like you."

It was my turn to bristle. "You assume I'm a scholarship student because I'm Mexican?"

"No," he said, "because you told me so last night." He smiled. "You said it as if you were proving a point to me."

"I thought you were another rich preppie here on his daddy's money."

His smile faded. "I haven't seen my dad in ten years."

"Does the woman you're engaged to mean anything more to you than the ones you went out with in college?"

"You've really got a mouth on you," he said. "You'll do well in court."

"Does she?" I persisted.

"No," he said. "I like her. I like her a lot."

"Her name's Bay? Like the body of water?"

"Asshole," he said, but he laughed when he said it. "Yes, Bay, Bay Kimball," he said. "She's a senior at a Catholic girls' school over in Marin, St. Clare's. Her father's Joe Kimball, the senior partner at the firm in L.A. where I clerked the last two summers. Awesome guy, Henry. I met Bay at a firm picnic. We both play tennis, so we played some and since we're both at school up here, I'd meet her in the city sometimes." He folded his hands behind his head. "I have to admit I kept in touch with her at first mainly because I really wanted an offer from the firm, and I figured it wouldn't hurt if I was friends with Joe's daughter. But after I got to know her, I liked her for herself and I could tell she really liked me. By the time I went back to the firm for my second summer, we were definitely dating."

"Someone who didn't like you as much as I do might say you're kind of an opportunist, Chris."

He moved away from me and said, "I know what you're thinking. I marry the senior partner's daughter and I can write my own ticket. You just have to trust that I'm not that much of an asshole. Look, Henry, try to understand. I knew I was homosexual when I was fourteen years old. When I was in high school, I used to bike to the library across town and look up everything I could find on the subject. All the books said I'd grow out of it. I waited and waited, but that didn't happen. I didn't want to be different, Henry. I still don't."

"You think getting married will change you?"

"God, I hope so," he said, in a voice so full of hurt that it made me ashamed for a moment of who I was.

"You think it's wrong to be gay, Chris?"

"It's wrong for me," he said.

"Maybe I should leave."

"I wish you wouldn't."

"You're a very confusing guy," I said.

"Are you so sure of yourself?" he asked me.

"No," I said, and I stayed.

•   •   •

After I talked to Captain Closet, I called Josh, but his line was busy. I tried again a half hour later, but it was still busy, so I decided to drive to West Hollywood and check on him. My route took me past Azul, the restaurant where Zack said he worked. I pulled into the empty parking lot. A handwritten sign on the door said "Closed Due to Act of God" and there was a number for emergencies. I jotted it down and headed west on Sunset.

The light glittered through the warm, hazy air and I pretty much had the road to myself. The traffic lights were out and businesses were shuttered, but the only visible damage from the quake was a few cracked walls. This hadn't been the big one, the cataclysm that was supposed to drop us into the Pacific, leaving only wisps of smog as a memorial to the city of the angels.

No doubt, a few thousand people would move on to stabler ground, and for a while those of us who remained would be more conscientious about our earthquake preparedness kits. Eventually, though, new residents would take the places of those who'd left, and the rest of us would forget to change the batteries in our flashlights. You need a short memory to live in L.A. That, and a blithe indifference to your own mortality. But for me, it was a city of death.

In the past few years, a dozen friends of mine had died from AIDS. I'd sat the watch with many of them. It sometimes seemed to me that I was living in one of those South American countries ruled by colonels, where people disappeared from the streets into the backseats of blue Fords, never to be seen again. The streets were haunted with their absence and there were rips in the fabric of my reality that could not be mended by grieving or the passage of time. And now the cars were coming for Josh.

Josh Mandel was the friend I thought I'd found in Chris Chandler all those years ago. I'd had to wait a long time and stumble into a lot of blind alleys before I found him. I'd been thirty-six, a recovering alcoholic fresh off his last binge and trying to get back the legal career I'd very nearly succeeding in drinking away. He was twenty-three and HIV-positive. Definitely not your traditional family, more like a couple of outcasts. They say love is blind, but only to convention. We saw each other clearly enough. Then he started to get sick, and decided I couldn't understand, and he left me for someone who could, and now he was even sicker, and his friend had died, and we could see each other again.

I pulled up in front of the brightly painted apartment where Josh lived. The front wall was orange, the beamed walkway to the street purple. Josh called it the HIV Hilton, because it had been built by the county to house people with AIDS. I rang the bell to his apartment, and a second later, a buzzer let me in. I crossed the courtyard and climbed the stairs to the third floor; inside the building, the colors were more subdued, pastel greens and blues. There was, as usual, little apparent activity and the quiet had the lassitude of a sickroom. Not all the tenants were sick, but, like a home for old people, a certain mortal inevitability hung in the air.

The door to Josh's apartment was ajar. I stepped inside and called out, "Josh."

He came to the door in a heavy robe. "Have you been trying to call me?"

"Yeah, but your line was busy."

"I know," he said. "My parents called, then my sisters, then my second cousin twice removed. Everyone was rallying around the fag."

"Are you all right?"

"Bushed," he said. He embraced me. I felt the lightness of his body beneath the robe. Had he lost more weight? It was hard to tell. Over the past year, his T-cell count had dropped into single digits and he had suffered from arrhythmia, diarrhea, fevers, disorientation, thrush, CMV and a bout of pneumonia. He had lost twenty pounds from his already slender frame and he exuded a faint chemical smell from all the drugs he took.

"Anything break in the quake?" I asked him.

He moved away. "I lost Steven," he said.

Since Steven was dead, I wondered if he was slipping into dementia, but then I followed his gaze across the room to the bookshelf where he'd kept a ginger jar containing Steven's ashes. It was gone.

"He fell and broke," Josh continued. "I swept up most of the ashes but some of them got in the carpet. You're probably stepping in him."

I lifted my shoe and inspected the sole. No Steven. "What did you do with the ashes?"

"I put them in a mason jar. I was about to scatter them." He turned toward the bedroom. "Will you help me?"

"Now?"

"I should've done it a long time ago," he said, "but I couldn't let go." He looked at me, frowned. "I'm sorry. I don't mean to hurt your feelings."

"My feelings aren't hurt," I lied.

I followed him through the bedroom to the small balcony where the jar of ashes rested on the railing. On the street below, papery bougainvillea blossoms swirled in the tail wind of a UPS truck. Josh clutched the railing with one frail hand while, with the other, he emptied the jar. I leaned over, watching the cloud of ash disperse in the luminous air, and thought, what a strange day. I felt Josh's thin fingers graze my hand.

"All flesh is grass," I murmured. "All its goodness like flowers of the field. Grass withers, flowers fade when the breath of the Lord blows on them."

"Isaiah," Josh said. "How do you know that?"

"Someone read it at Tim Taylor's memorial last month. It stayed with me."

"I remember it from Hebrew class," Josh said, and spoke a fragment of Hebrew in which I recognized only the word for God.

"What was that?"

"The beginning of the Kaddish." Then he laughed, the old, sharp yelp of a laugh.

"What's so funny?"

"Stevey was an Episcopalian. I hope his God understands Hebrew." He grunted.

"What's wrong?"

"The neuropathy's killing me today," he said. "My feet feel like they're on fire."

"Come inside, I'll massage them."

"Good-bye, Steven," Josh said, looking back at the dazzling emptiness of the air.

Josh slipped off his bathrobe, revealing boxer shorts patterned with ants, and lay down on his bed. His fine bones were clearly visible beneath sallow skin. His buttocks hung loosely, the muscle tone gone, and his genitals were sunken and limp. His once-sculpted chest and firm belly sagged, and he hunched his shoulders like an old man. I thought about all the times I'd made love to this body and how the vitality had seeped away from it, like a light burning out.

His face had thinned, but otherwise it was the thing least changed about him. I could still see, without too much squinting, Josh as he had been seven years ago; a boy of twenty-three with green eyes and lucent skin. I remembered the first time I had held him naked against my own naked body, the erotic shock that had passed through me, bringing me back to the life of the senses after so many years of living in my head, like someone starving in the garret of a mansion. Now his body reminded me that grief, like love, was also physical, and my body would have to grieve every detail of Josh's dying.

I poured a little baby oil in the palm of my hand and began to work his toes. They were curled from the neuropathy, an arthritic-like condition that affected his joints and made movement torture. He rarely complained about it.

"That feels good," Josh said. "Was your house okay in the quake?"

"Just a little broken glass. It didn't get really weird until after the quake."

"What do you mean?"

I told him about Zack Bowen.

When I finished, he said, "I'm sorry for Bay. I liked her."

"She liked you, too," I said. "She asks about you whenever I talk to her."

"I'm sorry about Chris, too," he added, tactfully. The two of them had taken an instant dislike to each other and for that reason we'd rarely seen the Chandlers when the two of us had lived together. "What are you going to do?"

"Find Zack before the police do, if I can. Help him."

"Even if he killed Chris?"

I kneaded his foot. "I don't think he did."

"How can you know that?" Josh said. "You just met him."

"He seemed kind of helpless to me."

He chided me. "Henry, you're such a sucker sometimes."

"Look, Josh," I reminded him, "I've defended dozens of murderers. You develop a sense about whether someone's capable of it or not. Zack didn't seem the type. He was too—I don't know, passive," I said, repeating my earlier thought. "More like a victim than a perpetrator."

After a moment, Josh said, "You said he was good-looking."

"I don't see what that has to do with it."

"Chris fell for him," Josh said, slyly. "And he was an older guy, too. Like you."

"Thanks a lot."

"You go for that type, Henry. The little bird with a broken wing."

"Now you're being a jerk," I said.

"When you find him, bring him to me. I'll tell you if he did it."

5

Josh fell asleep while I was massaging his feet. I covered him with a blanket, then went into the living room and called the number I'd written down from Azul. After a half-dozen rings, a distracted male voice said, "Yello."

"Hi," I said, "I got this number from the door at Azul. I'm trying to get ahold of Zack Bowen. I understand he works there."

"Just a minute," the man said. I heard him shouting at someone to get the door. "This place is a fucking madhouse. Now what did you want?"

"Zack Bowen," I said. "Do you know him?"

"Well, who is this?" he demanded.

"My name is Henry Rios," I said. "I'm a lawyer and it's very, very important that I find Zack."

A pause. "Is he in trouble?"

"I just need to talk to him."

"I don't give out information about my employees."

"I'm a criminal defense lawyer," I said, "and this is very serious."

"Look, even if I did give you Zack's phone number, it's not going to do you any good. He lives out in the valley, right where the quake hit, and I've been trying to call him myself. The phones are still out."

"What's your name?"

"Milt. Milt Harriman, and I'm really stressed right now."

"Give me his address, Milt. If I find him, I'll tell him you're looking for him."

Another pause. "How do I know you're on the level?"

"You'll have to take my word, Milt. If you don't, you'll be creating some big problems for Zack."

"Okay, okay," he said, and rattled off an address.

I left a note for Josh, telling him I'd drop by tomorrow, and headed over Laurel Canyon into the valley. It was five in the afternoon. In the past fourteen hours, I'd survived an earthquake, learned that one of my oldest friends had been murdered from his secret boyfriend and helped spread the ashes of the man for whom my lover had left me. Now I was passing through a neighborhood of little houses behind white picket fences, with children's toys scattered across carefully tended yards. I felt like Oscar Wilde in the suburbs.

This is what Chris had meant when he said he didn't want to be different. He wanted that white-picket-fence domesticity, the safety of fitting in, a map to living. Being gay meant being exiled from that ordinary world, banished to the fringes where you met a lot of fringe people in some pretty dubious situations. At least that's what it had seemed like twenty years ago to a couple of naive gay boys trying to figure out how to become men. I couldn't really stay mad at him for the choice he'd made, especially after I'd met Bay.

I met her at a party in someone's backyard, a couple of months after Chris and I had started sleeping together. It was just after winter finals and the place was packed with haggard law students intent on getting drunk and possibly laid. Music blasted from inside the house, shattering the surrounding suburban silence. The yard was littered with plastic cups, and another keg had just been tapped. I was wandering around half drunk when I heard someone calling my name. I looked around, and saw Chris coming out of the house holding hands with a blonde girl. My instinct was to walk the other way, but the tide was against me and I was pushed toward them.

"Henry," Chris said, "I want you to meet Bay. Bay, this is my friend, Henry, I've been telling you about."

"Hi," she said, extending a hand. "It's nice to meet you. Chris is always talking about you."

"Hi," I said, awkwardly shaking her hand.

"I'm going to get a beer," Chris said. "You want one, Bay? Henry?"

He was gone before either of us could answer. Bay had the fresh, shiny prettiness of the children of the rich; pink and gold skin, white, even teeth, her blue eyes clear and unclouded. She wore loose jeans and a heavy cable sweater, frayed a bit at the sleeves and the collar. They were the clothes someone wore to hide extra weight, but I could see it in her rounded cheeks and the hint of a double chin. Cruelly, I wondered what Chris saw in her besides a ticket to normality.

"So," I said, patronizing her, "you're a junior somewhere?"

"St. Clare's," she said, smiling a bit, taking my measure. "Why do law students feel so superior? My dad's a lawyer. It's nothing to be proud of."

I liked her for that. "You don't think so? Why?"

She shrugged. "Think about it, Henry. What do lawyers actually do except make money at the expense of other people's misery?"

"I guess that's why we feel superior."

"Chris said you had a sense of humor."

"If you have such a low opinion of law students, why are you engaged to one?"

"He's different," she said. "Don't you think so?"

I told myself to be careful. "Different? I'm not sure what you mean."

"He's not mercenary," she said, "and he's not arrogant and he's not boring."

"And you're in love with him," I said, drink getting the better of discretion.

"Hopelessly," she said, not altogether ironically.

"Is that from a movie? It sounds like something Claudette Colbert would say about Clark Gable. 'I'm hopelessly in love with him.'"

If she detected the mean-spiritness in that remark, she didn't let on. She laughed and said, "You're funny, Henry."

"No, just sort of drunk."

Just then, Chris reappeared, carrying three cups of beer. "Here you go," he said, handing them out. "You two getting along?"

"I like Henry," Bay announced. She took a delicate swallow of her beer and wiped her lip with her sleeve.

Chris glanced at me and said, "Good."

Some vintage Supremes came on and people started dancing. Bay grabbed my hand and said, "Let's dance, okay? I've been cooped up in the library all week."

"What about me?" Chris said.

"You, too," she said. "Come on."

We pushed our way to the middle of the yard and started dancing together. Her moves were fluid and uninhibited, as she turned now toward me, now toward Chris, hips swaying, breasts bouncing. Her face was flushed, and beads of sweat appeared on her forehead. She pushed her heavy hair back from her face and grinned at me. I felt awkward and self-conscious as I tried to keep up with her while staying clear of Chris, who bobbed up and down between us. After a few minutes, I shrugged and left them at it. I watched them from the edge of the yard. She danced toward Chris, who danced back at her. I could see from the way their bodies moved what they were to each other, and whatever fantasy I had entertained about Chris and me was dispelled at that moment. I went inside.

I found some people in the kitchen playing a drinking game that involved long strings of law Latin and a fifth of tequila. I was drunk when Bay caught up with me at the front door.

She tugged at my sleeve and said, "You're not leaving, are you? We hardly got to talk."

Her face was flushed and her eyes bright with drink.

"I thought you wanted to dance," I said.

"Chris got hijacked by his Moot Court partner," she said. "Stay and keep me company."

"You must know a lot of the people here."

"His other friends are so dull," she said, grinning. "You're not dull."

"How can you be sure?"

"Because you're gay," she said, merrily, and then her face went an even deeper red. "Oh, God, I'm sorry. I shouldn't have said that."

Even drunk, my guard went up, and I tried to pass it off as a joke. "The antonym for dull is exciting, not gay."

"I'm sorry, Henry. I say stupid things when I've had too much to drink."

I shrugged. "It's not a secret. Did Chris tell you?"

"He knew I wouldn't care," she said. "I have lesbian friends at school."

"It's all right, Bay," I said, zipping up my jacket.

"Don't go. You're the only one of Chris's friends I've met that I like. So naturally, I humiliate you. I feel awful."

"I'm not humiliated," I replied. All I wanted was to get away.

"Chris will be really upset with me for offending you."

She was near tears. I looked at her, and an alcoholic sentimentality descended on me. She ceased being the *femme fatale* of my imagination who had stolen Chris away from me. She was two or three years younger than me, just a child in my book, who wasn't holding her liquor very well, in a roomful of people she hardly knew. I slipped my hand into hers, feeling big and confident and protective.

"Come on, Bay, let's go dance."

"You're not mad," she said, with transparent relief.

"Not even a little," I assured her.

We went and danced.

Remembering that first time I met Bay, it occurred to me that I'd just met someone else who reminded me a little of what she'd been like then. Zack Bowen.

My search for Zack had taken me deep into the valley, beyond the '50s-fantasy suburbs into a dystopian sprawl of faded apartment complexes, warehouses and strip malls featuring fast-food restaurants that offered teriyaki burritos and drug transactions in the parking lots. For the first time I saw visible evidence of the quake, tumbled-down walls, shattered windows, the charred but still smoking remains of a row of stores. Police cars, fire engines and ambulances whizzed by. I drove past a scruffy little park where a bank of news vans from the local TV stations were lined up one after another in front of a tent village. Traffic was heavy and slow, and up ahead there was a police checkpoint where people were being turned around. I inched my way up to it. A uniformed cop stopped me.

"Sir, are you a resident of this neighborhood?"

"No," I said. "I'm looking for a friend of mine who lives around here."

"I'm sorry," he said, "from this point on we're just letting residents in."

"Is there any way I can just go and check up on him?"

"Sorry," the cop said, and gestured me to U-turn around his patrol car.

I turned around, drove a few blocks and parked. After consulting my map, I set off on foot to find Zack. I got as far as the block where he lived, where I was stopped again by another cop. His car blocked the street, and beyond it was a mass of people and emergency equipment.

"Sir," the cop said, "can I help you?"

"I'm looking for a friend of mine," I said. "He lives on this street at eleven-forty-eight."

The cop said, "I'm sorry, but we're not letting anyone in here."

An ambulance roared by, its siren deafening. "What's going on?"

"One of the buildings collapsed," he said. "Not the one you're looking for. There're still people inside."

"But my friend," I started to say.

"Sir, everyone has been evacuated from this neighborhood. You're not gonna find him." While he spoke to me, he waved a news van through. "Take my word for it."

"Where were they evacuated to?"

"Various locations," he said.

"Can you be more specific, Officer? I'm really worried about him."

"Try that little park up on Shakespeare. Then there's the high school over on Caldwell. Those are your best bets."

I went back to my car and drove to the little park I'd passed earlier. I spent the next hour picking my way through hysterical children and shell-shocked adults, and then I drove to the high school, where I searched the gym for another hour. I was feeling pretty shell-shocked myself by the time I left there, having given all the money I had, and a pint of blood, to the Red Cross people who were running the place. But I didn't find Zack. Finally, bone-tired, I gave up, went home and slept for fourteen hours.

6

THE EARTHQUAKE DOMINATED THE FRONT SECTION OF THE *TIMES* the next morning, pushing Chris's murder to a brief article on page 3 of the Metro section that reported that Chris had been "bludgeoned to death" by an "unknown intruder." The one detail that interested me was that the weapon had not been found at the scene. Zack had told me differently. I called Captain Closet and reached him just as he was leaving for work.

"That's right," he said about the missing weapon, then paused. "Do you know what it was, Henry?"

"No," I said.

"I'm getting a little tired of this one-way street," he said.

"You wouldn't have found Chris if I hadn't called you," I pointed out.

"If you're protecting his murderer . . ." he began threateningly.

"No," I said sharply. "This is called representing a client."

"Fine. Then get your information through the usual channels, Counsel." He slammed the phone down.

I stood there with the receiver in my hand. I'd been thinking about the weapon that Zack had described as a marble pyramid, trying to remember the objects in Chris's chamber. And then it came to me: a green marble obelisk that had been given to him earlier in the year by the county bar association as an award for being trial judge of the year. He used it as a paperweight. A sick joke. Zack said he'd left it there. Where was it? And where was Zack?

I called Milt Harriman's number.

"Hello," a male voice, not his, said groggily.

"Is Milt there?"

"He's at the restaurant. Do you want to leave a message?"

"No, thanks."

I showered and dressed. As I was driving to Azul, I thought about the weapon again. Trial judge of the year. Chris was very proud of that award. I wondered if the murderer was trying to make an obscure point by using it. All I could think of was that it was some dissatisfied litigant come back to take an ironic revenge. Maybe I'd been wrong not to tell Captain Closet about the weapon. I'd have to think about it.

There was a silver Lexus in the parking lot of Azul. I pulled up next to it, got out and went to the front door. It was locked. I walked around to the alley in the back. The back door was open behind the screen door, and I let myself into the kitchen. It had been tossed around some, but there was no major damage.

"Milt," I called, entering the main dining room.

It was an elegant room, the chocolate brown walls lit by bronze wall sconces, smallish metal tables scattered across a concrete floor that had been painted deep blue and then lacquered and buffed to a mirror-like reflectiveness. Off to the side was a small bar. It was from there that a short man in khaki pants and a wrinkled white shirt, dark-haired, handsome and in need of a shave, came out holding a baseball bat threateningly.

"Who are you?" he demanded.

"Henry Rios. I talked to you yesterday about Zack Bowen."

"Oh, yeah," he said, letting the bat fall. "Sorry, Henry. We had looters during the riots. You find Zack?"

"I couldn't even get near his apartment building," I said. "It was across the street from the one that collapsed."

"Yeah, I saw the picture in the *Times*."

"I was hoping you could tell me who might know where he is, like family or something."

He squinted at me. "You look familiar, Henry. You eat here?"

"Once or twice," I said. "I'm sort of in the neighborhood. I'm surprised you remember."

"A memory for customers is essential in this business. I have some coffee in the bar, and about a thousand dollars' worth of broken cocktail glasses. Come on, I'll pour you a cup. Of the coffee, I mean."

I followed him into the bar. A big pile of broken glass had been swept up against the wall. He poured two cups of coffee and sat down at the bar with me.

"Why are you looking for Zack?" he asked.

"Did you know Zack had a boyfriend?"

"The way you say boyfriend you must be gay," he said. "Straight guys choke on the word, if they can bring themselves to use it at all. Yeah, I knew he had a boyfriend. Older guy named Chris. He came in a couple of times."

I tasted the coffee. It was spicy but good. Sort of like Milt Harriman, I thought, deciding to level with him.

"Chris Chandler was a Superior Court judge," I said. "Night before last, someone murdered him. Zack showed up at my door to tell me because Chris and I were friends, then Zack split before I could get the whole story out of him. I'd like to find him before the cops do and hear the rest of it."

"Wow," Milt said. "You think Zack did it?"

"I never met Zack before yesterday. You know him. Do you?"

"No way, Jose," he said decisively. "Zack's a nice kid who's had a rough life. The only person he ever hurt was himself."

"Why do you say that?"

"Look, all I care about is that my waiters show up for their shifts, smile pretty at the customers and do their job. Zack's great that way. I never asked him about what he did before he came to work for me, but after a while you get to know people's stories."

"What's his?"

"He was a street kid. I guess he hustled on the boulevard a little."

"How did he end up here?"

"Sam Bligh," he said, pouring me another cup of coffee. "You know him?"

"Nope."

"Maybe you aren't gay," he said, grinning. "Sam Bligh runs Wilde Ride Productions, purveyor of fine gay porn. Somehow Zack got hooked up with him, made a couple of videos, I guess, but didn't like the life. Sam asked me to give him a job. I started him out as a busboy and promoted him in no time. He's been working here a couple of years."

"Are you saying Zack did blue movies?"

He did a slow double-take. "Blue movies? Hello, it's the nineties, Henry. Porn's big business and Sam's like, I don't know, the Spielberg of gay porn. If Zack did work for him, it was definitely a step up from selling himself on the streets."

"The Spielberg of porn," I said, turning that notion over in my head. "Okay. And you hired Zack on his say-so. Why would a respectable guy like you be doing favors for a pornographer?"

"Sam brings me a lot of business," he said. "I cater most of his shoots. And why the attitude about porn, girlfriend?"

"I'm old-fashioned, I guess. So what about Zack? You know where I can find him?"

"No, he doesn't have family around that I know of. But Sam might know. They stayed pretty tight. I'll give you his number."

He went behind the bar and took out a Rolodex crammed with cards. He wrote out Bligh's name and number and gave it to me.

"Thanks, Milt, and if Zack does show up, will you tell him I need to see him? Tell him it's either me or the cops."

"Will do, Henry," he said, accepting the business card I handed him. "And if you're gonna see Sam, watch what you say about porn. He's kind of a crusader."

I didn't know what to make out of Zack's association with Bligh, but I could imagine how it would play in the media; murdered judge's porn star boyfriend. This information and the missing murder weapon made it more important than ever that I get to Zack Bowen. I called Bligh's number from my car phone, en route to Josh's apartment.

A male voice answered. "Hello."

It was Zack Bowen.

"Zack," I said. "This is Henry Rios."

A pause. "How did you find me?"

"That's not important. I have to talk to you."

"You were going to call the police," he said, accusingly.

"No, I told you I wasn't. You have to trust me, Zack."

"Why?" he demanded.

"Because you're in trouble. It's just a matter of time before the police figure out who you are and they'll be looking for you."

"Who's going to tell them?"

"People know about you and Chris," I said. "Your boss at Azul, for one. And Bay Chandler, or didn't Chris tell her about you when he left her?"

"He told her," he said. "He said they had a fight. It was really bad."

"The cops have probably already talked to her," I said. "They might already be trying to find you."

"What should I do?" he asked fearfully.

"Go to them first," I said. "I'll go with you. Tell them what you saw when you went to Chris's courtroom yesterday."

"They'll think I killed him."

"If and when that happens, we'll deal with it then," I told him. "You're only making it worse by running."

He breathed unsteadily into the phone. "I'm afraid."

"Zack, if you didn't do it, you don't have anything to be afraid of."

"I didn't do it!" he shrilled.

"Okay, then let's go to the police and help them find who did. Where are you now? What's the address?"

"I need some time to think," he said.

"We don't have much time."

"I need to talk to Sam."

"Sam Bligh? What's your relationship with him?"

"He's my friend," he said, defensively.

I didn't want to scare him off, so I dropped it, for now. "Okay, you talk to Sam. When can we meet?"

He drew a deep breath. "Later," he said. "I'll meet you at midnight at that coffeehouse on Robertson. The Abbey? You know where it is?"

"I'll find it," I said. "Zack, you're doing the right thing."

"You'll go to the police with me, right?"

"Yes," I said. "And Zack, one last thing. The story about Chris in the *Times* this morning said the police didn't find the weapon that was used to kill him. You said you left it there. You have any idea what happened to it?"

"No," he said. "It was there when I left."

"Well, give it some thought. I'll see you tonight. All right?"

"All right," he said, sounding relieved. "All right, I'll see you."

I put the phone down. It was just after eleven. Twelve hours until I met him. All I could do now was hope he actually showed up.

No one answered at Josh's apartment. Worried, I let myself in with my key and found the place empty. I looked at the calendar in the kitchen where he wrote down his medical appointments, and saw that he was scheduled for a visit to his doctor at eleven. Ordinarily, I drove him to his appointments, but sometimes he cadged a ride from a friend. I left him a note asking him to call me when he got home. Then, because I'd been avoiding it all morning, I called Bay Chandler.

The maid answered. I asked for Bay, and she said, "Mrs. Chandler's not talking to nobody but family."

"Would you just ask if she'll talk to me?" I said. "Henry Rios."

"Wait," she said, and put the phone down with a thunk.

A moment later, Bay came on the line. "Henry," she said. "I'm glad you called."

I was in an awkward position, possessing, as it were, insider information. I didn't want to deceive Bay, but I didn't want to upset her either, nor, until I talked to him again, did I want to implicate Zack Bowen in Chris's murder.

"I read about Chris in the paper," I said, truthfully. "I'm so sorry. Is there anything I can do?"

A pause. "No," she said. "I mean, I don't know. Sorry, the police were just here. I've been answering their questions all morning and I'm not thinking very clearly."

Hesitantly, I asked, "Do they have any suspects?"

"No," she said. "I wasn't much help to them. Henry, you talked to Chris sometimes. Do you have any idea of who . . ." her voice trailed off. "The last time you saw him, did he say anything to you?"

"No," I said. "I had coffee with him a couple of weeks ago. He seemed fine."

"He wasn't worried about anything?"

"Not as far as I could tell," I replied. "Was something wrong?"

"That's what the police asked me," she said. "I couldn't think of anything."

"Nothing at all?" I asked, thinking if, in fact, Chris had left her for Zack Bowen, and they'd quarreled, there would've been plenty of things wrong.

"Nothing," she said, in a whisper. "I'm very tired, Henry. Will you excuse me? Can we talk later?"

"Of course," I said. "I'll call you tomorrow, is that all right?"

"Yes, please," she said. "Good-bye."

I put the phone down and compared the two conversations I'd had, with Zack and Bay. They didn't mesh. One of them was lying.

7

WHEN I PULLED INTO MY DRIVEWAY A HALF HOUR LATER, I NO-
ticed a woman sitting in a car across the street. She got out of her car
at the same time I did and approached me. She was an almond-eyed
African-American, her skin the color of cinnamon. She wore a khaki
skirt and a black blazer over a plain white blouse. She radiated cool
authority. A cop.

"Mr. Rios?" she said, smiling at me. "I'm Detective McBeth from
Homicide. I wonder if I could speak to you for a moment?"

"Do you have some identification?"

Her smile narrowed as she reached into her skirt pocket and withdrew a wallet, which she opened to a badge and an identification card.
I pretended to study it. Her name was Yolanda McBeth.

"All right?" she asked me, closing the wallet.

"What can I do for you?"

"I wanted to talk to you about Judge Chandler."

Captain Closet having his revenge, I thought bitterly. He must have
revealed that I'd reported the murder. I decided, on principle, to be
uncooperative.

"What about him?"

"He was found murdered this morning in his courtroom," she said.

Warily, suspecting a trap, I nodded. "I know, I read about it in the
Times," I said. "It's unbelievable."

I waited for her to say something about my call to Captain Closet,
but she merely nodded agreement. "Nowhere seems to be safe anymore."

"I don't know why you want to talk to me about it," I said, truthfully, surprised she'd passed up a chance to catch me in a half-truth about my knowledge of Chris's murder.

"You represented Judge Chandler in a lewd conduct case up in San Francisco about fifteen years ago," she said. "I wanted to ask you a few questions about it."

I tried not to reveal my astonishment at the turn in the conversation, but said, as blandly as I could, "Why don't you come inside, Detective?"

I left her in the living room while I went into the kitchen to make coffee, a pretext to give me a moment to think. It appeared she didn't know I'd called Captain Closet to report Chris's murder. On the other hand, she knew about Chris's arrest, something I was certain he'd never revealed to anyone and as to which there was only the sketchiest of records buried deep in the bowels of the criminal justice system. I'd seen to that. Whoever this woman was, she was formidable.

When I went back into the living room with the coffee, she was standing at the fireplace, examining a black-and-white photograph of me and Josh, his arm around my shoulders, mine around his waist.

"Nice picture," she said, with a warmer smile than the one outside. "Your friend is very handsome."

There was just enough innuendo to make it clear that she understood the nature of the relationship captured in the photograph.

"I'll tell him you said so," I replied, handing her a cup of coffee.

"Thanks," she said. She sipped it. "This is nice. Kona?"

I sat down. "Is this supposed to catch me off my guard?"

She sat down in the chair across from me. "Why should you be on your guard?"

"How did you find out about the lewd conduct case?"

She grinned and said, "It wasn't easy, Mr. Rios. I ran a routine computer check to see if Judge Chandler had any kind of record. The only thing I could come up with was this old conviction for disturbing the peace. It seemed out of character for someone as respectable as the judge, so I contacted San Francisco PD and had them fax me the police report. When I discovered that the arrest had been for lewd conduct, I obtained the court docket to see who the clever lawyer had been who'd managed to plea-bargain it to a four-fifteen. That led me to you."

"I'm impressed," I said. "You're better than the FBI, though I don't understand why you ran his record in the first place."

"I do it on all my cases," she said. "Sometimes you find a skeleton or two in the closet that might help explain an otherwise inexplicable murder."

"A skeleton in the closet," I repeated. "What are you implying?"

"Judge Chandler was arrested for soliciting an undercover police officer," she said, all business now. "A male officer. Was he gay, Mr. Rios?"

"Anything he told me at the time of his arrest is privileged information," I replied.

She sipped her coffee, eyes narrowed in thought.

"According to Mrs. Chandler," she said, "you and the judge were friends in law school."

"That's true," I conceded.

"And you're gay," she said.

"Did Bay tell you that?"

She shook her head. "No, I found that out for myself by doing a computer search of your name on the *Times*'s on-line service," she said. "You've handled some high-profile cases. There was a feature about you a few years back. You're not in the closet."

"You are good, Detective," I said. "But there's a flaw in your logic. The fact that I'm gay and Judge Chandler was a friend of mine doesn't mean that he was gay."

She put her cup down. "Mr. Rios," she said. "Let's stop playing games. Judge Chandler was brutally murdered last night. If he was gay, there may have been a connection between his sexual orientation and the murder."

"Such as?"

"Maybe he picked up the wrong person last night and brought him back to the court and things got out of hand."

"I bet you didn't try that theory on Bay Chandler," I said.

"Mrs. Chandler didn't know anything about the judge's lewd conduct arrest," she said, grimly. "You can imagine her surprise."

I didn't say anything. I was more confused than ever now, because if Chris had left Bay for Zack, she could hardly have been completely surprised at the nature of Chris's earlier arrest. Somebody, either Zack or Bay, was lying.

"She was surprised by the arrest or your suggestion that Chris was gay?" I asked.

I saw too late that it had been the wrong question to ask.

"Shouldn't she have been surprised to find out he was gay?" she asked me.

"Detective," I said. "I represented Chris in the one case. As far as I know, it was an isolated incident. As for your theory of who killed him, all I can say is he never told me he was out there picking up guys and bringing them back to his courtroom for sex. And if he had, surely someone would've noticed. A guard, a janitor." I shrugged. "I can't help you."

She held her silence until it began to get awkward. I knew this trick, however, and said nothing.

"Mr. Rios," she asked, "do you know a man named Zack Bowen?"

"No, who is he?"

"His name appeared frequently in the judge's personal calendar, the one he kept in his desk at the court. His number was in the judge's Rolodex, also at his office, but not the one he kept at home. Mrs. Chandler had never heard of him. I ran his record. He has a half-dozen arrests, mostly juvenile, all for prostitution. Ring any bells?"

"No," I said.

She frowned and stood up, smoothing her skirt. "Why would someone like Judge Chandler befriend a hustler?"

"I don't know," I replied.

"I think you do," she said. She moved to the fireplace and picked up the picture of Josh and me. "Being out of the closet is a luxury that many gay people can't afford. Maybe you can't understand that, but it's something I think about." She put the picture down and looked at me. "If Judge Chandler paid for being in the closet with his life, I'd think you'd want to help me find his killer before another gay man pays the same price."

"Are you trying to tell me you're a lesbian?" I asked her.

"I'm trying to tell you I think we have a common interest here," she said. "You're a criminal defense lawyer. You know the drill in a homicide investigation. There are always two detectives assigned to a case."

"And you're here on your own," I said.

"I can promise you discretion," she said.

"I'm sure you could," I replied, "but I can't help you."

"Thank you for the coffee," she said. "Here's my card. Call me if you think of anything that might help my investigation."

I tucked the card into my shirt pocket. "I'll do that."

"Appreciate your time," she said.

I smiled insincerely. "No problem."

She was no sooner out the door than the phone rang. I picked it up, still running my conversation with McBeth through my head, and it took me a moment to recognize the woman's voice on the line saying, "Henry, it's Selma Mandel." Josh's mother. She and his father lived in Claremont, about an hour's drive east. She said, "I called you earlier, but you were out. I'm afraid Josh is in the hospital again. They took him this morning."

"What happened?"

"He woke up having trouble breathing. He's here at Midtown."

"I'm on my way," I said, and only then did I notice the half-dozen messages on my answering machine from the morning.

The fourth floor of Midtown Hospital—the AIDS ward—had become as familiar to me as the floor plan of my own house. Once I'd come to visit one friend and bumped into another strolling down the hall, dragging his IV along with him. My AA sponsor, Tim Taylor, had died in one of these rooms in a hospital gown and handmade Italian slippers. He'd left them to me. I could neither wear them nor throw them out, so they gathered dust in the back of my closet.

Josh was sitting up in bed with an oxygen mask pressed to his face, watching *The Simpsons*. His mother, Selma, sat in a chair beside the bed, knitting. I kissed him on the forehead.

Selma said, "Hello, Henry."

"Hi," I said. "How are you feeling, Josh?"

He lifted the mask long enough to say, "Like shit."

"That's the spirit," I said.

Selma got up. "Sit down, Henry. I need to call Joshua's father."

"Tell him I'm okay," Josh said.

She kissed his cheek. "Don't talk too much."

After she left, I sat on the edge of the bed and reached for his hand. "Is it pneumocystis?"

He flicked the mask to his forehead impatiently. "They don't know," he said. "They shot me up with antibiotics just in case. I'll just be here a couple of days, but now Dr. Singh thinks there's something wrong with my kidneys—" He pulled the mask down, took a couple of deep breaths and lifted it again. "I'm backing up, like a broken-down toilet."

"What's he recommend?"

"More drugs," Josh said, disgustedly. "I swear to God, it's the drugs that are killing me, not the infections. I cannot take one more thing. Next I'll be wearing diapers and—" He pulled the mask down and breathed, gripping my hand. When he raised it again, he said, "I can't do this anymore."

"We'll get through it, Josh."

"What's the point," he said, tears gathering in his eyes. "It's not like I'm ever going to be well again."

I squeezed his hand and repeated, helplessly, "We'll get through this."

He wiped his eyes on his sleeve and nodded. "Stay with me a while, okay?"

"I'm not going anywhere," I told him.

He closed his eyes. Within a few minutes, he was asleep. I got up and went to the window. The Century City towers glittered through the hazy late October afternoon. There was laughter in the hall behind me. I said a prayer, always the same prayer. Two words. Help us.

"He told me he doesn't dream anymore."

Selma was standing in the doorway, a plump woman in late middle age, her heart-shaped face drawn and tired.

"Probably he just doesn't remember them," I said.

She approached the bed. "I used to think it was unnatural that Josh is a homosexual," she said. "Now I know that unnatural is when a child dies before his parents." She smoothed the sheets above his wasted legs. "I wonder, have we done right by him? Given him enough support?" Her voice shook. "What is enough in a situation like this?"

"You've been wonderful," I said, and added, tactfully. "Sam, too."

"Sam tries, Henry."

I nodded. Josh's father had never come around to the fact either that Josh was gay or that he had AIDS. I still hadn't forgiven him for a remark I'd heard him make to Selma the last time Josh was in the hospital. "My boy is dying of a homosexual disease," he'd said. "Just what every father hopes for."

"Sam's stubborn," Selma said. "So is Joshua. Stubborn and sensitive. I used to think maybe he'd be an artist of some kind." She picked up her knitting and carefully put it into a canvas bag. "But I was afraid for him, too. The world's a hard place for men who are stubborn and sensitive. But you know that." She squared her shoulders. "Now that you're here, I can go. I'll be back in the morning."

"I'll see you then," I said.

For the rest of the evening, Josh drifted in and out of sleep. We talked while he was awake, and when he was asleep, I held his hand and thought. Not about him or us or the future. That was too big and frightening a place to go to. I thought about Chris and Bay and Zack Bowen and Detective McBeth. My conversation with her had confirmed that Bay either didn't know about Zack Bowen or wasn't telling. If she knew about Zack, if, in fact, Chris had left her for him, why would she not reveal that to the police? Zack said that she and Chris had fought over his leaving. Was she afraid if she said something it would cast suspicion on her? Bay a suspect in Chris's murder? The notion was incredible. Yet, when I thought about the manner of the murder, the weapon, the violence, it had all the markings of a crime of passion, improvised and ugly. And Bay was nothing if not passionate.

8

I LEFT JOSH AT AROUND 10:30 AND RAN INTO HIS DOCTOR, VIKRAM
Singh, coming out of another patient's room. Singh was a small, slender man, whose dark, fine-boned face was set in deep lines of fatigue.
He saw me, extended a slim hand and said, "I was just going to look in
on Josh," in an Anglo-Indian accent that made even the most banal
greeting sound like a line from the Upanishads.

"He's asleep," I said. "You're working late."

He shrugged. "We should talk. Let's go into the common room."

The common room was dominated by a wide-screen TV and big
framed photographs of movie stars. Bookshelves held paperbacks and
board games. There was track lighting and modular furniture in pale
blues and greens. It was spotlessly clean, as if it had never been used.
With a sigh, Singh slumped into an armchair.

"You know Josh is very sick," he said, the harshness of the words
blunted by the softness of his voice.

"Does he have pneumocystis again?"

He shook his head. "No, it's not PCP this time. Just a mild case of
ordinary pneumonia. That wasn't what I meant when I said he's very
sick."

"Then what?"

"His kidneys are beginning to fail," he said. "It's called HIV-
nephropathy and it leads to a condition called uremia. Do you know
what that is?"

"He told me he was like a backed-up toilet."

Singh smiled briefly. "It's good he can still make jokes. What it means is that his bloodstream retains the toxins that are normally excreted in the urine. Eventually the system poisons itself."

"What can you do?"

He gave me a look at once sympathetic and irritated. "There's really nothing," he said. "Not in his condition."

"And what is his condition, exactly?"

"Well," he said, "as you know, he went through a period of neurological disability early on and there's still some impairment there, loss of short-term memory and some minor motor problems, but he's still functioning at a very high level of mental acuity, all things considered. That could change, of course. His main problem is the MAC, the wasting."

"I know what that means."

"Yes," Singh said, wearily. "The weight loss, the diarrhea, fatigue, insomnia, all those symptoms. His neuropathy is also getting worse, bad enough that he may soon have trouble walking. All this has left him very, very weak."

"How weak?"

"He's entered a terminal stage, Henry. He may have a few weeks, a few months, but no more than that. I think it best for you to prepare yourself."

My heart seized up, and for a moment I couldn't answer. "Have you told his family?" I asked, finally.

Singh looked puzzled. "I was under the impression that you are his family."

"I meant his parents."

He shook his head. "I've had very little contact with them. I thought it should come from you or Josh."

"You've talked to him?"

"We had a long talk the last time he came in to see me," he said. "He asked me to talk to you. He thought you might have questions for me. Do you?"

"Can he manage on his own or should I make him move in with me?"

Singh smiled and said, "I think we both know one doesn't make Josh do anything he doesn't want to. He's all right where he is for now. Later, yes, you may want to try to persuade him to move. Failing that, we can arrange round-the-clock nursing, but we're not there yet." He touched my hand. "This is difficult." It wasn't a question.

"What did he say when you told him?"

"He said he had no idea that dying would be such hard work," Singh replied.

I went down to my car, got in and sat, waiting for something to happen, some tidal wave of grief or anger to overwhelm me, but all I felt was a kind of dazed fatigue. It was the mental emptiness of effort I used to feel when I was a distance runner on my high-school track team, and everything got reduced to putting one foot in front of the other.

What was I then, fifteen, sixteen, pounding the dirt path along the river that ran through my home town? I sought refuge in that emptiness from my first awareness that I was different from other boys. What had Chris told me about his own adolescence, that he didn't want to be different? I didn't, either. I watched my classmates being initiated into the world of men and women where everything was planned and the outcomes known; marriage, children, family. That world was closed to me. I didn't have a plan, didn't know where I would end up or with whom. So I ran, mile after mile, until my body ached and my mind went blank.

What happened is that I realized I could not outrun this thing. I remember that day, staggering along the path after a stupendous effort, darkness falling in the summer sky, racked with the dry heaves, gasping, "I'm a queer," the only word I knew for my condition. I was full of fear and I felt completely alone, but I could not deny the truth and there was a kind of relief in that.

I had now reached the same point with Josh's disease. I couldn't outrun it. "He's going to die," I said, testing the words. They had the same ring of the truth as those other words I had spoken to myself all those years before. I felt the same relief that I had felt then, but now I understood its source. The truth can be painful, but it does not produce evil. Lies are the source of evil. With that thought in mind, I went off to meet Zack Bowen.

The Abbey was on Robertson, just below Santa Monica, on the edge of Boys' Town. Low brick buildings housed cafes, clothing stores, coffee houses and watch repair shops that rubbed elbows with gay clubs and sex shops. These establishments catered to hordes of the beautiful young gay men who lived in the big apartment complexes that lined the side streets or who drove in from all over Southern California on weekend nights. I seldom ventured there, because it reminded me San Francisco in the '70s, when I was a boy just coming out and how out of place I'd felt among the big-muscled boys who cruised each other with cold assessment. Twenty years later, only the faces and the clothes had changed; the air was still charged with the brutal calculation of lust. And beneath that was the claustrophobia of a ghetto, of fearful people looking out at the world from behind invisible fences. On a wall near West Hollywood Video someone had spray-painted, Free Fag Zone, but it wasn't any kind of freedom I understood.

The nearest parking I could find was several blocks away, and as I walked back to the coffeehouse I passed a video store. I went in and asked the girl at the counter, "I wonder if you could help me. I'm looking for movies from an outfit called Wilde Ride Productions."

"They'd be in adult videos," she said. "Last aisle. Are you looking for one in particular?"

"I don't think so," I said, feeling rather sheepish.

"Well, they're shelved alphabetically by title, but you tell from the spine of the box who the production company is."

"Thanks," I said.

"No problem."

Ninety percent of the adult videos were gay and there were a lot of them. It wasn't clear to me whether I was looking for a clue to Zack Bowen's character or if I just wanted to satisfy my prurient curiosity, or both. I glanced at the first couple of shelves, looking at the spines of the video boxes until I found one from Wilde Ride. It was called *Asshole Buddies*. I pulled it from the shelf and studied the cover. There was a glossy photograph of two naked young men, pink and muscle-bound, standing back to back and leering at me. I turned the box over. There were smaller pictures of other young men, their names written beneath them. One of them was called Nick D'Angelo, and it was Zack Bowen. He was sitting in a chaise lounge, a swimming pool glittering behind him, wearing a tiny bathing suit. He looked younger than I remembered him, and when I checked the date of the movie it was from three years ago. I put it back on the shelf and left the store.

It was a quarter to twelve when I got to the Abbey. It was set back from the street and opened up to a big courtyard dominated by an enormous iron statue of Mercury. The courtyard was half full of men sitting in small groups around metal tables, talking, playing board games, drinking coffee, watching each other. I bought a cup of coffee and found a table near the entrance and waited.

I waited for an hour, until the courtyard was nearly deserted and the boys behind the counter were beginning to put things away. Then I got up and headed back to my car. The video store was still open. I thought about the movie I'd looked at earlier, *Asshole Buddies*. I didn't know what it would tell me about Zack Bowen, if anything, but on impulse I went in and rented it.

There was a message from Bay Chandler on my answering machine when I got home. She'd left it that morning, before McBeth dropped in on me. She said, in worried tones, "Henry, this is Bay. I talked to a police detective after you called, a black woman named McBeth, I think. She told me something very disturbing about Chris that I need to talk to you about. Please call me as soon as you get this message." There was another message from her, from around ten. "Henry, it's Bay again. I really must speak to you. Could you drop by tomorrow morning, around ten? If you can't come, please call me first thing in the morning." This time, there was just a trace of anger in her voice. I could guess what she wanted to talk to me about. Chris's lewd conduct arrest. I erased the messages.

I went into my bedroom and popped the video into the VCR, got undressed and into bed and pushed Play on the remote control. An American flag appeared on the screen, flapping gently in the breeze, and a deep, masculine voice made a pitch for the First Amendment. "Remember," he said, as the strains of the *Star Spangled Banner* played softly in the background, "censorship is un-American." Then the flag dissolved to a scene of two young men fucking in the back of a pickup truck while the credits ran. I fast-forwarded, missing, I'm sure, the intricate plot and witty dialogue, until I came to Zack's scene.

He pulled himself out of a swimming pool and toweled himself off, then retired to the chaise longue where, conveniently, someone had left a dildo. He performed various autoerotic acts with it and then another boy, one of the two pink musclemen from the cover, came upon him. He talked streams of juvenile smut while he yanked Zack's legs over his shoulders and began to fuck him without a condom. Except for their genitals, their bodies did not touch. The pink boy muttered things like "Take my big dick, faggot," while Zack grimaced and blinked the sunlight out of his eyes. Otherwise, his face revealed nothing, but it was the nothing of someone whose mind was elsewhere. When they finished, they jumped into the pool, and then the film cut to the next scene. I rewound the tape.

That night I had a long, complicated dream that ended with me being drunk. When I woke up, the only other thing I could remember about it was that Josh and Bay had both been in it. Afterwards, I couldn't get back to sleep, so I pulled on a pair of sweatpants and went into the kitchen to make a cup of tea. As I poured water into the kettle I glanced out the window. Across the street, a man sat in a parked car smoking a cigarette. I took my tea out to the terrace. The smell of jasmine seeped through the chilly air. I only dreamed of drinking when

I was anxious, my unconscious seeking the relief that I no longer permitted my conscious self. I knew it was about Josh but also, thrown into the mix, was the guilt I felt over deceiving Bay.

We hadn't really become friends until after Chris had graduated from Stanford and moved to Los Angeles to work at her father's firm, while she returned north to finish her last year of college. I was finishing my last year of law school. At first we saw each other because we had in common that we missed Chris, but then we discovered another shared interest: we both liked to drink.

When Chris was still around, I would go out with them from time to time. The three of us went through many bottles of wine together, Bay and I easily outdrinking Chris. I never gave it a second thought. After Chris left, Bay and I were a little shy in each other's company and it took a few drinks to relax us. Soon enough, drinking became a central, if unspoken, reason for our get-togethers. We released something in each other because, except when I was with her, I rarely drank, and from what she told me I gathered it was the same with her. Sober, she was a quiet girl of twenty who made self-deprecating remarks about her weight and her intelligence, but after a few drinks an entirely different person inhabited her body: a smart, sensual woman who could be bitingly shrewd and funny. Drinking with her took on an aura of romance.

We'd meet in the bar of a second-class hotel on Geary. It was dark and deserted, with a jukebox that played Billie Holiday and Dinah Washington. The bartender was an Australian and a dead ringer for Elizabeth Taylor in a fat phase, who poured drinks with a heavy hand. In a booth upholstered in worn red leather we'd listen to old songs suffused with that warm alcoholic glow that lifted us out of the ordinary and made everything bigger and more dramatic.

One night she insisted that I take her to a gay bar.

"Why?" I asked warily.

"I want to see that part of your life."

"It's not that interesting."

"It would be to me. Please, Henry, I'll behave."

"It's not a stop on the Gray Line tour."

"I don't want to gawk," she said, offended. "I want to size up the competition."

"What competition?"

"The competition for you," she said, smiling provocatively. This was a familiar line of banter between us.

"You're almost a married woman," I pointed out.

"Almost, Henry, almost. Come on, I hear the best dancing in the city's at gay bars."

"Cha-cha-cha," I said, and we were off.

The Hide 'n Seek was, as usual on a Saturday night, packed and smoky, musky with sweat and cologne. In the darkness, Bay grabbed for my hand and whispered, "I can hardly breathe in here."

"You'll get used to it," I said, pumping her hand reassuringly.

I got us drinks and edged her against the wall near the dance floor where the boys moved like liquid sex to the throb of disco. A tiny blond sashayed past us, stopped, looked at Bay, touched her breast and said, "Nice drag, honey."

"It's real," I said.

He yanked his hand back as if burned and went on his way, laughing.

"Was he making a pass at me?" Bay asked.

I explained drag to her.

"He thought I was a boy?" she giggled. She looked around the room. "I wish I was a boy tonight. These guys are gorgeous."

"Looks aren't everything," I told her.

"No? What do you want in a man?"

"Don't be a bitch."

"I'm serious," she said. "You never talk about your boyfriends. What are they like?"

"I don't have one," I said.

"But if you did, what would he be like?"

Like Chris, I thought. "Oh, Bay, I don't know. I'm just looking for that certain special anyone. Let's dance."

I dragged her out to the dance floor, where we wedged ourselves among the dancing boys. She was as snaky-hipped as they were. I watched her move, studied her body, tested myself for responsiveness. But it was the boy in the tight black jeans behind her who raced my pulse.

"What are you thinking?" she shouted over the music.

"Not thinking," I said. "Dancing."

She pressed against me, her breasts soft on my chest, her hair swishing against my cheek and said, "Don't I turn you on, just a little?"

"I'd have to be dead if you didn't," I replied.

She smirked. "Liar. My tits terrify you."

"Yeah, they're pretty scary," I agreed.

And we both laughed.

At last call we were sitting on empty beer boxes against the wall, watching the boys frantically pick each other up.

Out of nowhere, Bay asked, "Did Chris ever cheat on me?"

"Why are you asking?" I replied, neutrally. "Do you think he did?"

"No, not Chris," she said. "Maybe I want him to. Maybe I want him to fall in love with someone else. Maybe I don't want to get married."

"No? Why not? Don't you love him?"

"He's just so safe," she said. "I want an adventure."

"Who's stopping you?"

"The only time I feel free is when I'm with you," she said, leaning against me. "Are you sure you don't want to sleep with me?"

I put my arm around her and marveled, in my twenty-three-year-old way, at the irony of the situation.

"I'm sure," I said.

I finished my tea and went inside. Bay and Chris were married eight months later at a church in Pasadena. They wrote their own service

and she asked me to help her find a poem to read. I gave her some
lines from Whitman:

> I give you my love more precious than money,
> I give you myself before preaching or law;
> Will you give me yourself? Will you come travel with me?
> Shall we stick together as long as we live?

9

THE NEXT MORNING, BEFORE I LEFT FOR BAY'S, I CALLED SAM Bligh's number. The man who answered was not Zack Bowen, but I recognized the voice, deep and mellifluous, as the same one condemning censorship as unAmerican on *Asshole Buddies*.

"Hello," he said.

"Mr. Bligh?" I guessed.

"That's right. Can I help you?"

"My name is Henry Rios. I need to talk to Zack Bowen."

A pause. "I'm afraid Zack's not here."

"He was yesterday," I said. "I spoke to him. He was supposed to meet me last night, but he didn't show. Maybe you can tell me why."

"No," he said, in his deep rumble, "I don't think I can help you, Mr. Rios."

"Mr. Bligh, I'm a criminal defense lawyer. Zack is in a lot of trouble, but I assume he's already told you that. The police have already been around to see me once, but I fended them off. I can't continue to do that if he won't talk to me."

"I see," he said. "What did the police want with Zack?"

"I think you know that, too. Let's stop playing games."

"You'd better come around then," he said.

"I have another appointment this morning. I could come after that. Where are you?"

He gave me an address. "Let's say one-thirty," he said.

I agreed and hung up.

•   •   •

As I drove to Bay's, I wondered how much McBeth had told her about Chris's arrest fifteen years earlier. I had only the vaguest recollection of the arrest report, but I remembered in great detail the night he'd called me from jail. It had happened five years after Chris and Bay were married. I was working in the Public Defender's office in Palo Alto. I had only seen Chris and Bay a couple of times after their marriage, but Bay wrote once or twice a year. She always enclosed pictures of Joey, who'd been born a year after they'd married. She seemed unhappy, and I thought I discerned the effects of alcohol in her long, rambling letters. I scribbled postcards in return. From Chris I heard nothing until that night.

It was a little after three in the morning. I picked up the phone and mumbled, "Hello."

Even before the caller spoke, I knew from the background noises—clanging metal, shouted commands—that I was being called from a jail.

"Henry," a man said. "It's Chris Chandler. I'm in the San Francisco jail. Can you get me out?"

His voice drove the fog from my head. "Chris? What happened?"

"We can talk about that later," he said brusquely.

I sat up in bed. "I'm not asking out of idle curiosity," I said. "It's relevant to whether I can get you out."

"Lewd conduct," he answered. "Are you coming?"

"Don't talk to anyone until I get there," I said. "I'm going to make a few calls and see if I can't get you out on your own recognizance. If they release you before I arrive, wait for me outside. Got that?"

"Thanks," he said, in the same short-tempered tone. "I'll wait for you."

I called a D.A. acquaintance in the city. He roused a judge, who agreed to let Chris out O.R. As soon as I heard back from Mike, I got dressed and drove to the jail. Chris was waiting outside beneath a street lamp. I pulled up to the curb and opened the passenger door. He came toward me walking like a barefoot man across a bed of broken glass. He got into the car and slammed the door shut.

"Are you okay?"

He was disheveled and his eyes were bloodshot. He smelled of liquor.

"Fuck," he said, pounding his fist against the dashboard. "Fuck, fuck, fuck." Then he began to sob.

I put my arm around his shoulders and he buried his face in my chest. When the sobbing eased up, I asked him, "Where are you staying?"

"The St. Francis," he said, sitting up and wiping his face on his sleeves. "Thanks for coming, Henry."

"No problem," I replied, and started up the car.

An hour later we were sitting at a table in Chris's suite, plates of untouched food between us. A window looked down on Union Square where flocks of pigeons peppered the faded winter grass. Chris had showered and changed, but still looked awful.

"Eat something," I told him.

"I'm not hungry," he said. He reached for a cigarette from the pack on the table. The ashtray was already overflowing. "I guess you want to know what happened."

"I can't help you unless you tell me."

He exhaled a snake of smoke. "It's funny being the client instead of the lawyer." I said nothing, waiting for him to gather his courage. "Yeah, okay. Yesterday I was in deposition from nine in the morning to six at night. After that I had dinner with the client, who screamed at me for two solid hours about our bills. Then I came back here and called Bay and we had a fight over Joey's bedwetting." He drew on the cigarette. "She wants to take him to a shrink. The kid's only six."

"Tell me about the arrest."

He smirked. "Just the facts, right, counsel? Okay. After I hung up on Bay I went down to Polk Street to the P.S. and got drunk. I haven't been to a gay bar in five years, but I went just like that." He snapped his fingers. "Didn't even stop to think about it. As I was sitting at the bar, a blow job began to seem like a really good idea. I didn't want to pick up anyone there. I didn't want conversation. I remembered that park, the Buena Vista. There was always a lot of action in the bushes. You been?"

"It's not my scene, Chris."

"No, of course not," he said. "Anyway, I drove to the park and started walking around. This guy stepped out from some tall bushes playing with himself. I went over and helped him out and then two other guys came out of nowhere and threw me on the ground. I thought I was being mugged. Then one of them said, 'You're under arrest, faggot.' They handcuffed me and put me in a police car with a couple of other guys. They took us to the jail and booked us. After that, I called you."

"When the first guy, the cop who came out of the bushes, when he approached you, was his penis out of his pants?"

"His penis? Henry, he was jerking himself off."

"What was the conversation?"

Chris looked away. "He said, 'Looks good, doesn't it.' Then I said, 'Looks good enough to eat.' "

"And did he say anything else?"

Chris looked back at me. "He said, 'Go ahead.' That's when I touched him." He drank some water. "That's it."

"There're the makings of a very good entrapment defense here."

"Are you crazy? I can't go to trial. I'm up for partner in my father-in-law's firm. I've got a kid. There's Bay."

"Are you willing to plead guilty?"

"I can't do that, either."

"Okay," I said. "You don't want to go to trial, but you don't want to plead straight up. So here's your only other option—bargain the charge down to something innocuous, like disturbing the peace, and cop to that. It'll stay on your record, but you can lie about it. One more lie won't hurt you."

"Don't be so fucking sanctimonious."

"I noticed you didn't call your father-in-law to get you out of jail."

"What's that supposed to mean?"

"You're like those closet fags who keep a gay doctor in reserve for when they pick up the clap at the bathhouse. You called me because you assumed I'd keep your secret."

He glared at me. "That's so easy for you to say. What do you know about my life? It doesn't matter to you that I've been a good husband and a good father. Well, fuck you, Henry. My wife loves me, my boy loves me, and I've earned that love. I don't deserve your contempt because I made a mistake." He stubbed out his cigarette, making a mess of it because his hands were shaking. "Until last night, I haven't gone out on Bay since we got married," he said. "Most of the time I think I'm over it and then I'll see someone and I'll feel this intense sadness." He drew a deep breath. "I still think about you. I still wonder what it might have been for us. Maybe that's why I called you last night. I don't care if you don't believe me."

After a moment, I said, "I believe you, Chris. I'm sorry if I was out of line."

"Don't you ever wonder about us?"

"There's nothing to be gained by it."

"No," he said, thoughtfully. "I guess not. You probably have a lover."

I shook my head. "No, I don't. You were right about that, Chris. It's not so easy to find someone, not for more than sex, I mean."

"It doesn't sound like being out of the closet is much better than being in it," he said.

"That's what you never understood," I said. "I didn't come out to improve my chances of finding a boyfriend. I came out because I had to."

"Would you change who you are if you could?"

"Have you?" I asked him.

He avoided my eyes. "Can you get the charge reduced, Henry? Will you do that for me?"

"Yes," I said, "I'll take care of it."

In the end, Chris pled to disturbing the peace in front of a fierce old judge named Atlas Angeloni who called him a pervert after he read the arrest report. It must have been the most humiliating day of his life. I wasn't surprised when I didn't get a thank-you note.

The Chandlers lived in Pasadena on a winding, tree-lined road of quiet affluence. It was the kind of neighborhood that didn't have sidewalks and employed private armed security patrols. At the corner was a bus stop where a bus came twice a day to deliver and remove the maids. The big, rambling houses combined elements of Spanish Mission and English Tudor in a bland melange of white stucco and exposed beams, lapped by deep lawns the color of money. They reminded me of the opening lines from Yeats's poem about the Irish Civil War: "Surely among the rich man's flowering lawns,/Amid the rustle of his planted hills,/Life overflows without ambitious pain . . ." I thought of neighborhoods in the city, blighted by drugs, poverty and violence, the houses more like bunkers than habitations. The houses to which the maids returned. The ugly, cheap apartment buildings in the valley, like the one that had collapsed in the earthquake across the street from where Zack Bowen lived. Life overflowed there, too, but it was more sewage than rainwater. A slow-motion civil war was taking place all over the city; it needed only a spark to combust. Some of the people who lived in these great houses were aware of that, Chris and Bay among them, and they did what they could. Me, too, for that matter. The ones who were honest about it knew it wasn't enough.

I pulled into the driveway at the Chandlers' house behind a black Jeep Cherokee, went up to the door and rang the bell. The door opened and Joey Chandler stood looking at me with his father's pale eyes. The resemblance didn't end there. At twenty, he was Chris in miniature, having inherited his father's features, but not his height, being no more than five-eight. In the last couple of years, he had taken up weight lifting and built himself a heavy, hyperbolic body that he inhabited without grace.

Joey had always been an anxious and difficult boy. As a child he'd been given to sudden, destructive rages. While these had abated when he reached adolescence, he still gave the impression of deep and abiding fury. Bay blamed his emotional disorders on her drinking when he was a child. Maybe that was true, but I sometimes wondered if Joey hadn't also absorbed some of his closeted father's ambivalence, because Chris worked at fatherhood with an intensity that seemed driven by guilt. When I'd once said something like this to Chris, it was as if I'd accused him of being a child molester and I never mentioned it again.

Whatever the cause, Joey was not a likable boy.

"Hi, Joey," I said. "I'm so sorry about your father."

He glanced at me indifferently and said, "She's in the kitchen."

Before I could respond, he turned and walked away.

I stepped into an octagonal foyer. There was an Oriental carpet of deep red on the parquet floor, and in the center of it a rosewood table on which a big blue vase held white carnations. An archway opened to a wide hall. At the end was a grand staircase. The faint spicy smell of the carnations pervaded the still air. I remembered Chris's pride the first time he had shown me through the house, as if it was a museum to his success, while Bay, who had grown up rich, had been quietly but distinctly embarrassed.

I made my way through the richly furnished rooms to the kitchen, where I found Bay on the phone. She saw me and smiled sourly. Her face was pale and she wore no makeup. There were tight lines across her forehead and around her mouth. She had long ago dieted and exercised away her schoolgirl fat, achieving a society-lady thinness that was accentuated rather than hidden by the baggy jeans and loose white tee shirt she wore. There was, in fact, little left of the boozy college girl with whom I'd once danced in the gay dives of mid-'70s San Francisco. This woman radiated a hard-won self-assurance. I poured myself a cup of coffee from the silver thermos on the marble-topped island in the center of the bright kitchen and walked to the French doors at the end of the room. They opened out to the garden and the swimming pool, where Joey sat, his massive back to me, staring at the water.

Bay finished her conversation and hung up the phone.

"Hello, Henry," she said, coolly.

I walked back to her and kissed her cheek. "Hello, Bay. How are you doing with all this?"

She lit a cigarette from the pack on the counter, exhaled a furious cloud of smoke and said, "You bastard."

10

"YOU WANT TO EXPLAIN THAT?" I ASKED AFTER A MOMENT.

"How long did you know about Chris?" she demanded. "Why didn't you ever tell me?"

"That he was gay? Is that what you mean, Bay?"

She stubbed out her cigarette. "I trusted you," she said. "I confided in you, and all this time you lied to me. How do you think it felt when that policewoman told me that Chris had been arrested in the bushes with another man? You knew about that, you knew about this other thing, this fling of his. How many others were there, Henry?" Her hands shook. "What kind of friend are you?"

"It wasn't my place to tell you," I said.

She flushed, her face tight as a mask. "But you knew," she said sharply.

"It was never that simple," I replied. "What Chris told me about his sexuality changed over the years, but I know he was always committed to your marriage."

"Until he left me," she said bitterly.

"I didn't find out about that until a couple of days ago," I said.

"I don't believe you."

"It's the truth, Bay. As far as I knew, Chris was faithful to you except for that one incident in San Francisco."

"When married men cheat on their wives, it's usually with another woman," she said. "Why did he go into that park? Why did he call you?"

"He told me he knew he was gay from the time he was fourteen," I told her, "but he didn't want to be. He wanted a family, stability, a career, things he didn't think he could have if he was gay. He also loved you. That's why he married you. He made a choice, Bay, a conscious, deliberate choice. I didn't think I had the right to interfere."

"You could have warned me."

"Warned you about what, that someday he might leave you for someone else? Isn't that a risk that everyone assumes when they live with someone else?"

"It's not the same," she said. "If he'd left me for another woman, he would've still been the same person, but when he left me for this other man, it was as if I'd never known him."

"Man or woman, I don't see the difference."

"Do you know what he told me?" she said, the bitterness creeping back into her voice. "He said he needed to be loved by that person in that way. I was so angry, I could have killed him myself."

"And then someone did," I said.

She caught her breath. "What do you mean by that?"

"Have you told the police that Chris left you?"

She avoided my eyes. "No."

"I didn't think so," I said. "McBeth, the homicide detective who talked to me, didn't seem to know. Why didn't you tell her, Bay?"

She fumbled for a cigarette. "It's humiliating," she said. "It's not something I want people to know."

"These aren't just people," I said. "These are the police. It's just a matter of time before they find out. They're already searching for Chris's friend. It won't look good when they find out that you withheld that information from them."

"I don't understand," she said, nervously raising the cigarette to her mouth.

"Chris left you, and shortly afterwards someone killed him. There's a motive there."

She stared at me aghast. "You think I . . ."

"I'm only telling you what it's going to look like to the police."

She shook her head violently. "That's absurd. If anyone had a motive to kill Chris, it was that man."

"Zack Bowen? Why?"

"Chris left him money," she said, angrily. "He changed his will and made him a beneficiary."

That made me pause a moment. I hadn't been able to see Zack killing Chris in a fit of passion. But money made everybody do foolish things.

"Did you tell the police?" I asked.

"I didn't know until after they talked to me," she said. She glanced out toward the pool. Joey had got up and was walking toward the house. "You're right, Henry, it was a mistake for me not to have told the police that Chris had left me. I'll call them today. I'm sure they'll be interested to know about the will, too."

"How is Joey taking this?"

When she looked back at me, I thought I detected a glimmer of fear in her eyes. "He loved his father," she said.

"He didn't seem too broken up when he let me in," I started to say.

"I'm glad he's dead." Joey was standing in the doorway now, his hands balled into fists.

Bay said, "Joey!"

He came into the kitchen and drilled me with his pale eyes. "He was a faggot and I'm glad he's dead."

"I didn't know you felt that way about gay people," I said.

"He's upset, Henry," Bay said quickly. "He doesn't mean it."

Joey turned on her. "He ruined this family."

"Whatever he did, he didn't deserve to die for it," I said.

"What do you know?" he said contemptuously. "My dad, judge of the year. Fag of the year. That's what they should've given him the award for."

Bay hurled herself around the counter and slapped him. "That's enough."

He touched his face. "Fuck you," he shouted, and ran from the room. In the distance, a door slammed.

Bay slumped against the counter. "Do you mind going now, Henry? I think I've had enough for one morning."

"I'm sorry, Bay," I said.

"You can't blame Joey," she said, turning to me. "He's still furious with Chris for leaving. He doesn't understand yet that he won't be coming back."

It seemed to me she was talking as much about herself as her son.

When I went out to my car, I saw Joey sitting in the driver's seat of the Jeep. Something he had said in the house caught my attention. I went over to him. He stared straight ahead, his hands on the steering wheel. The key was in the ignition.

"Sorry," I said, "I didn't mean to block you."

"Are you leaving now?" he rasped.

"If you'll answer a question," I said.

He shifted slightly in the seat. "What?"

"Why did you say that about the award? The judge of the year award? Did you know your father was killed with it?"

His knuckles went white on the steering wheel, and when he answered there was a note of pleading in his fury. "Could you please let me out, please?"

I got into my car and backed out of the driveway. Joey darted out and skidded down the street, running the stop sign at the corner. I looked back at the house. Bay was standing at the door. I lifted my hand. She didn't wave back.

He knew, I thought. Joey knew his father had been killed with the award. It was on his mind, that was why he'd mentioned it in the kitchen. He was so angry that he probably wasn't aware of what he'd said until I asked him about it, and then he remembered that according to the paper, the weapon used to kill Chris was still unknown. And, in fact, according to Captain Closet, the police didn't know, so how could Joey Chandler know? Only if he had been in Chris's chambers the night he was murdered or had talked to someone who was.

I let the thought sink in. Bay hadn't told the police Chris had left her because she was humiliated by it, she said. I remembered my first conversation with her after Chris's death became public. When I'd asked her if Chris had been worried about anything, she said no, though I knew from having talked to Zack that Chris had left her. Was she too humiliated to tell me about their troubles? It wasn't like Bay to lie, nor was it likely that she wouldn't have figured out that her marital problems may have interested the police. She was, after all, both the daughter and the wife of lawyers. And this sudden mention of Chris having named Zack as a beneficiary in his will. That seemed improvised, as if to deflect suspicion away from her, or Joey.

Then it occurred to me that I was actually considering Bay or Joey as murder suspects, and the thought shamed me. Was Bay a liar? Wasn't I a greater one? Hadn't I failed to mention to her that Chris and I had slept together when we were students? Hadn't I forgotten to disclose that I not only knew Zack Bowen, but had talked to him the night Chris was murdered? I could try to rationalize my lies of omission as attempts to protect her from knowledge that would only make things worse for her, but that in itself was a lie. I hadn't told her about Chris and me because I was afraid to, I hadn't told her about Zack for the same reason. I was afraid to lose her friendship, but that didn't keep me from suspecting her of Chris's murder. She was right not to trust me.

I wanted to wash my hands of all of them, Chris, Zack Bowen, Joey, Bay, but it was too late for that. Twenty years too late. Now I would have to see it through.

11

I HAD TOLD BAY THE TRUTH ABOUT ONE THING: UNTIL ZACK Bowen had turned up at my door four days ago, I had had no reason to believe that Chris had been unfaithful to her after his arrest in San Francisco. I was thinking about that as I drove across town to the address Sam Bligh had given me, which was somewhere in the Hollywood Hills above the Sunset Strip. He wasn't expecting me for another couple of hours, but it occurred to me that I had a better chance of catching Zack if I turned up unannounced. The weather had heated up and there were low clouds in the sky, creating a humid, sour atmosphere. The aftereffects of the earthquake were still in the news, but now it was all about emergency relief and who was going to pay for it. As with most disasters in the city, the poorest neighborhoods were the hardest hit and the various levels of government were quick to disclaim any responsibility for them. The rest of the city had already begun to turn its attention elsewhere. It really was a brutal place, Los Angeles, less a city than a collection of hostile villages united only in their mutual suspicion of each other and a susceptibility to disasters, natural and otherwise. Fires, floods, riots and earthquakes; it was looking more and more like Armageddon-by-the-Pacific.

I had moved here reluctantly seven years earlier because Josh had wanted to be near his parents. I had known very few people and the prospect of starting up a new law practice had been daunting. Chris was a judge by then. I'd read it in our law school alumni magazine, because after what had happened in San Francisco, I lost all contact with him, and even Bay had stopped writing except for Christmas cards. At the time I hadn't thought much of it, because I was busily descending into the final stages of alcoholism; the place where I needed a couple of drinks in the morning just to get out of the house and judges were beginning to hold me in contempt because I forgot to show up for trials. That's another story. By the time I had arrived in Los Angeles, I'd been sober for a couple of years. I was trying to get my practice up and running, and I'd sent around announcements of the opening of my office. Chris called and asked me to drop by his courtroom. We hadn't talked to each other since we'd stood together in Judge Angeloni's courtroom and Chris had entered a plea of guilty to a reduced charge in his lewd conduct case. Neither of us mentioned it on the phone. One morning, after I finished an arraignment at the Municipal Court Building, I decided to look in on him.

He was off the bench. A small, dusty plastic Christmas tree decorated the clerk's desk in a cubicle adjacent to the bench. The clerk, a chubby black woman with bleached blonde hair, wearing a green sweater embroidered with a reindeer, regarded me suspiciously when I asked to speak to Chris. She finally agreed to let him know I was there, picked up her phone, whispered into it, listened, hung up and said, "Come through here."

She held open the swinging door that led into her cubicle and directed me to a door behind her that opened to a corridor. I passed through. The corridor was lined with bookshelves that held dusty volumes of the California Reporter, First Series, a collection of judicial opinions reaching back to the 1850s. There were doors at either end of the hall.

"To your right," she said.

I went down to the door with Chris's name engraved on a brass nameplate. The door was half open. I peered in and saw Chris at his desk looking back at me.

"Henry," he said, rising. "Come in."

"Hello, Chris," I said, entering the room.

"Shut the door behind you."

His chambers were modest. Built-in bookshelves held more recent volumes of the California Reporter and other legal treatises. A wan ficus stood limply in the corner. A door opened to a small, tiled bathroom. Thin muddy-colored carpeting covered the floor. The windows framed the criminal courts building across the street. His desk was plain and solid, identifiably the product of a prison woodshop.

"I expected something more lavish," I said, settling into a hard, wooden chair of the same style as his desk.

He grinned and said, "So did I. I was used to my corner office on the partner's floor over at Joe Kimball's firm."

"How low the great have fallen," I murmured.

"The interior decoration isn't the worst of it," he said. "The courthouse is a security nightmare. It was built in the fifties by the same firm that built a couple of the local state colleges. I don't think they understood the difference between a dormitory and a courthouse. There are so many ways in and out of this place that a couple of my colleagues carry guns. Since I was elected presiding judge, I've been trying to discourage that habit. It doesn't exactly instill confidence in the judicial system."

"I don't understand what they'd be afraid of. You don't try criminal cases in this building."

"You're new to the city," he said. "This is not a good neighborhood. There was a rape in the stairwell not six months ago." He dug into his shirt pocket and pulled out a stick of gum. "Nicotine gum," he said. "I've been trying to quit. You look great, Henry, but what happened to your hair? It's all gray."

"The same as happened to yours," I said. "Time."

He touched the receding line of his hair. "Yeah, well I'd rather have your problem than mine."

His face was heavier and more set that when I'd last seen him, and he was bulkier. A man's face, a man's body.

"It suits you," I said.

"I was really surprised to get your announcement. I figured you'd never leave the Bay Area."

"I figured the same thing," I replied, "until I fell in love with someone who lives down here."

"Ah, that's great. Another lawyer?"

"No. Josh is a student at UCLA."

He raised an eyebrow. "A student?"

"He's twenty-three, Chris, well past the age of consent."

"Of course it's none of my business," he said.

"Of course," I agreed.

"The last time I heard anything about you on the Stanford grapevine it didn't sound like you were doing too well."

"I wasn't," I said. "I was a drunk. I've been sober two years now."

"Congratulations," he replied, meaning it. "Bay's sober, too, you know, or probably you don't know. It's been four years now. I don't think our marriage really began until she stopped drinking."

"Good for her," I said. "I remember we both hit the bottle pretty hard when we were at school."

"I know she'd love to hear from you," he said.

I nodded. "Maybe I'll give her a call."

"Maybe?" he said, chewing his gum. "Why wouldn't you?"

"I don't want to lie to her," I said.

"Lie to her?"

"I assume you never told her about Buena Vista Park," I said. "She never mentioned it in any of her Christmas cards."

"God, this stuff is vile," Chris said, spitting the gum into a wastebasket. He opened his desk drawer and pulled out a pack of cigarettes and an ashtray. He lit a cigarette and inhaled. His face relaxed. "It's humiliating, isn't it? Being hooked on anything?"

"When you asked me to drop by," I said, "you specified your court. Why not invite me home to dinner, Chris? Were you afraid I'd say something?"

He dragged on his cigarette. "Let me ask you something, Henry," he said. "If someone's an alcoholic but he manages to stay off the bottle for a couple of years, don't you say that he's a recovering alcoholic?"

"Yeah, so?"

He put his cigarette out and slipped the pack and the ashtray into his desk. "Well," he said, "you might say I'm a recovering homosexual. I haven't cheated on Bay since that weekend. I've been a good father and a good husband, better than I was before. So you see, there's nothing to tell her."

"Because you're cured."

His mouth tightened, then he asked, "This guy you're with, Josh? How long have you been together?"

"Over a year."

"Do his parents know?"

"What is this, a deposition? Of course his parents know. Everyone knows. We're not hiding anything here. That's never been my style."

"I remember. Back at school you were always expounding on the virtues of being out of the closet, and I'd say, let's talk in twenty years. Well, here we are, coming on twenty years and you're a recovering alcoholic with a kid for a boyfriend. I can see what you mean about being out. It's so much better."

My face burned. "If that's what you have to think about me to make yourself feel better about deceiving everyone in your life, you're even more pathetic than I thought you were."

We glared at each other, and then Chris looked down and shuffled some papers.

"I see you're on the nine-eighty-seven panel," he said, referring to the criminal defense lawyers the county hired to defend indigent defendants. "I'll make sure you start getting appointments."

"Is this a bribe?"

"You always did see things in the worst possible light," he said. "No, it's not a bribe. I checked out your references. I understand you're a very fine lawyer when you're sober, and since that isn't a problem any more we can use your talent."

I looked away from him, past the smeared window to the balmy December day and thought about the uncertain state of Josh's health and how neither one of us had health insurance.

"I don't want your help," I said.

"You won't need it for long," he said. "Pretty soon you'll have more business than you can handle and we'll be even."

I looked back at him. "What are you talking about?"

"You helped me once, remember? You saved my career and possibly my family. I'm paying you back."

"And that's why you wanted to see me alone, to pay me back a debt you never told anyone you owed?"

"I'm trying to wipe the slate clean, Henry, so that we can be friends again."

"What about Bay?" I said. "Is that slate clean?"

"I would never do anything to hurt Bay or Joey. Would you?"

I took the 987 appointments he threw my way and I called Bay and we resumed our friendship and I kept Chris's secrets which, after a time, seemed less like secrets than youthful indiscretions. As I turned off Sunset onto King's Road, I suddenly understood that the reason he had not told me about Zack or leaving Bay was because of how hard he had worked to convince me that he had changed. He was a "recovering homosexual." It would have been as humiliating for him to admit to me he was involved with Zack as it would have been for a recovering alcoholic to admit he'd started drinking again. But maybe if he had told me, I could've helped him and he might still be alive.

I followed the winding roads up the hill, past low walls overgrown with bougainvillea, until I came to the address that Bligh had given me and parked at the end of his dead-end street. I walked back to the house, which was at the end of a driveway behind a locked gate set into a brick wall. I buzzed the intercom in the wall. A staticky voice, not Bligh's, said, "Hello."

"It's Henry Rios," I said. "I have an appointment to see Mr. Bligh."

The intercom clicked off and for a moment nothing happened. Then the front door opened and someone began walking toward me, a tall boy in a pair of faded gym shorts. He was blond and his skin was a deep golden brown. There was not an ounce of spare fat on his perfectly proportioned body. From a distance, he looked barely out of his teens, but when he came to the gate I saw he was much older, but in an undefinable way; his face showing not age, but wear. There was a touch of leatheriness to the skin and his mouth was bracketed by deep lines. Puffiness showed beneath his eyes, as if he had just awakened, and his eyes were narrow blue slits. His hair, I now realized, was bleached and the dark roots had begun to grow out. If his body belonged on a beach, his face would have been more at home in a bar, where the darkness would have erased its flaws and he could have passed for twenty-three. In the sunshine, with his mop of improbable hair, he looked a hard decade older.

"Mr. Rios," he said, in a soft, faintly southern drawl. "We weren't expecting you till later."

"I take it you're not Sam Bligh."

He showed me a mouthful of expensive orthodonture. "I'm Tommy Callen," he said. "Sam's assistant."

"My meeting finished early," I said, "and I was in the neighborhood. It seems pointless for me to drive home and then come back. Can I see Mr. Bligh?"

"He's in the middle of something just now."

"I won't keep him," I said.

His smile turned slightly feral. "It's really not a good time."

A voice crackled over the intercom. "Tommy?"

"Yeah, Sam."

"I need you in here," Bligh said.

"Mr. Bligh," I said. "I'm trying to explain to your assistant here that I only need a minute of your time."

"Who is that?" Bligh demanded.

"Henry Rios," I said. I looked at Tommy, who now wore a guilty grin. "Didn't Tommy tell you I was here?"

"What the hell's going on out there?" Bligh said.

"I'll take care of it, Sam," Tommy said, unlatching the gate. "Come on. I'll take you to him."

As we walked up the driveway to the house, I asked, "Why didn't you tell him it was me at the gate?"

"You'll see," he said, opening the door to let me pass.

•   •   •

There were mirrored walls in the small entrance hall that reflected a miniature of Michelangelo's David on a black marble plinth. Beyond that was a large, sun-filled room furnished in white. I could see through glass doors a terrace and a pool. The terrace was landscaped with potted palms and exotic flowers. The pool was an irregular circle, rimmed with porous stone. At the far end of the terrace, beneath a vine-laden gazebo, there was a sunken hot tub. It took me a moment, but I recognized the pool as the set in *Asshole Buddies.*

"Over here," Tommy said, walking ahead of me, through the white room.

I followed him into a smaller room dominated by an oversized TV on which a soundless video was running, showing half a dozen men having sex on board a boat. In the center of a room, watching the film, was a tall, powerfully built old man grasping the railings of a wooden platform, his legs encased in metal braces. Beside the platform was a motorized wheelchair. The platform was arranged at an angle so that I saw him in profile. He wore a red-and-white striped shirt and white slacks pulled tight by the straps of the braces around his wasted legs. He was bald, except for a fringe of long white hair, and he sported a goatee.

"Mr. Bligh?"

He craned his neck to face me. He was round-faced and ruddy. Beneath wire-rimmed glasses, his eyes were bright blue and he might have passed for a department-store Santa Claus but for the hooded intelligence in those eyes; they were the eyes of a bird of prey.

"Mr. Rios," he said, in his deep, booming voice. "You're early." He reached for a remote control on the railing and switched the TV off. "Get me down, Tommy."

Tommy Callen unstrapped him and helped him into the wheelchair. When he was settled, he said, "Sit down, Mr. Rios. Tommy, bring us some coffee."

I sank into an overstuffed chair. "I'm sorry. I didn't mean to intrude on your physical therapy."

"What, that?" he said, glancing at the platform. "It's not really therapy. It helps the circulation in my legs and it feels good to be upright
for a while, but it doesn't improve my condition."

"How long have you been in a chair?"

"Ten years," he said. "Industrial accident. I'll spare you the details,
but the settlement bought me this house and helped me start up my
production company. So I suppose it was a fair trade." His eyes
beamed irony. "Though I might have been asked first."

"You own Wilde Ride outright?"

"Lock, stock and barrel," he said.

"How does someone get into your business?"

He crinkled a smile. "You exude distaste, Mr. Rios, and that sur-
prises me after everything you've done for the community."

"What community is that?"

"The gay and lesbian community," he said. "I'm a big contributor to
a lot of the organizations, and after I talked to you I made some calls.
You're a contributor yourself. I'm surprised we haven't met before at
the Center dinner or an APLA party."

"Those functions seem awfully self-congratulatory to me," I said.

"And why shouldn't they be?"

"To congratulate yourself on your own generosity seems a little im-
modest, wouldn't you say?"

"I don't see it that way," he said, amiably. "I see it as a celebration of
our survival as a people."

"I'm not sure we would agree on who our people are," I said. "I've
seen one of your movies."

"And what did you think of it?"

"I'm a firm believer in the First Amendment," I replied.

"You disapprove," he said, lightly.

"It bothered me that your performers didn't use condoms."

"You're talking about *Buddies*," he said. Tommy brought in a tray
with coffee. He took a cup. "Thank you, Tommy." He offered me the
cup. "Sugar, cream?"

"Black is fine," I said, taking the cup.

"I didn't direct *Buddies*," Bligh continued. "The man I used thought the action would be hotter without condoms. I fired him when I found out, but he'd already shot the footage and it seemed pointless to waste it." He sipped coffee. "I value my actors. It was very upsetting to me." He set the cup down. "You asked me how I got into the business, Mr. Rios. I'll tell you."

"Please."

"Because I'm in this chair," he said, gripping the arms of his wheel-chair. "You see, someone like you, young, good-looking, able-bodied, can actualize his erotic fantasies. I can't. And there are more gay men like me in this country than there are like you. Not necessarily crip-pled, but closeted, maybe, or in small towns or living in the country, remote places where you can't find the sexual opportunities that exist in places like West Hollywood. My movies are their lifelines. I give them in fantasy what most of them will never be able to have in reality."

"But always the same fantasies," I said. "The same muscle-bound boy having impersonal sex."

He chuckled. "You don't understand how it works. The movies sketch situations, the viewer fills in the blanks. Isn't that what sexual fantasy is all about?"

"I've never fantasized about someone calling me a faggot while I was giving him a blow job."

He fixed me with his predator's eyes and said, "The thing that makes sex between men exciting is the implicit possibility of violence as their powerful bodies go at each other. It's as much about making war as making love. Your lover is also your enemy. Of course there's an ele-ment of humiliation in it. That's part of the erotic thrill."

"Someone else might say you promote self-hatred," I said.

"He would be wrong," Bligh said, icily.

"We'll have to agree to disagree," I said. "I didn't come here to talk about your movies. I came here to talk to Zack Bowen."

"He's not here, Mr. Rios," Bligh said. "He left yesterday."

"Where did he go?"

"Before I answer that," he said, "if I answer it, I need to know what your interest is."

"The police are looking for him in connection with a murder. He came to me asking for my help, then ran away before I could give it to him."

"Why would you want to help Zack?"

"I'm not sure I do," I said, "and I won't be sure until I talk to him, but better me than the police. The murder victim was a friend of mine."

"Judge Chandler," Bligh said, sedately sipping his coffee.

"You knew him?"

"I introduced him to Zack."

12

"I DON'T UNDERSTAND," I SAID. "HOW DID YOU KNOW CHRIS?"

Bligh raised his cup to Tommy, who had sat silently through the conversation. He poured coffee into it and gestured to me with the pot. I shook my head.

"I told you I'm a big donor to gay causes, but not just gay ones," Bligh said. "In this political climate, it helps to have friends in power. I met Judge Chandler at a fundraiser for the mayor a couple of years back. We got to talking and he was very interested in my line of work. The judge was one of those men I was telling you about earlier who don't have access to the gay world. I mentioned to him that I occasionally gave small parties where I introduced my friends to some of my actors. I asked him if he'd like to come to one of them. Of course, he said he would."

"What kind of parties?"

Bligh laughed, a great, booming laugh. "Dinner parties, Mr. Rios. Not orgies. Not with all the white in this house."

"I see," I said. "You introduced powerful, closeted gay men to prospective sex partners."

"I introduced one set of friends to another set of friends," he said. "Whatever else happened was up to them."

"You pimped your actors," I said.

"Do you know what, Mr. Rios?" he said smoothly. "I don't think I much like you."

"Maybe it's because I don't trade in the same euphemisms as you do."

He shrugged. "Whatever. I'm not running a prostitution ring. I just do favors for my friends."

"Friends who could do you favors in return," I said. "Friends who would have something to fear from you if they didn't return your favors."

He shook his head chidingly. "You have a devious mind. I suppose it comes from your legal training. Let me be clear, I'm not a pimp and I'm not a blackmailer. I'm a businessman in a very controversial business who watches out for himself."

"Was Zack a regular at your parties?"

"No," he said. "Zack worked for me."

"He performed in your movies, you mean."

"Just the one," he said. "He had the right look, but not the right attitude."

"What do you mean?"

"You said you saw the movie," he replied. "Did Zack look like he was having a good time?"

"No, he looked like he wished he was someplace else."

"Exactly," he said. "By the time I found Zack, he was pretty damaged. He was a street hustler, you know. That's not an easy life. Anyway, I couldn't use him in the videos, so I hired him to look after me, what Tommy does now."

I glanced at Tommy, who frowned but said nothing. A moment later, he slipped out of the room.

"It was generous of you to keep Zack on," I said.

"You have a gift for innuendo," Bligh rumbled.

"I'm just responding to what you don't say."

"What am I not saying?"

"Zack did more than look after you, didn't he? Wasn't he your lover, too? Isn't Tommy?"

"So?" he said, touching a withered leg. "Did you think I became a eunuch when I lost the use of my legs? There are other ways of having sex."

"That's not my point," I said. "Did Zack leave you for Chris?"

"He went with my blessing," Bligh said, with a crooked smile. "It was good for my business. I put my personal feelings aside."

"What happened then?"

"They fell in love," Bligh said. "I didn't hear from either one of them again until Zack showed up a few days ago needing a place to stay. He said his apartment was damaged in the earthquake, but then I read about the judge's murder and when I asked him about it, he told me everything."

"What did he tell you, Mr. Bligh?"

"He told me that he'd gone to the courthouse the night of the earthquake and found the judge already dead. Isn't that what he told you?"

"Yes," I admitted. "Did you believe him?"

"Zack doesn't lie," he said simply.

"Not even to protect himself?"

"Zack's problem," Bligh said, "is that he doesn't know how to protect himself."

Bligh's observation squared with my sense of Zack as being child-like.

"Why didn't he meet me last night?"

"Because I wanted to meet you first," Bligh said. "I wanted to make sure you didn't intend him any harm. Do you?"

"Why should I? He came to me."

"You were Judge Chandler's friend. If you think Zack killed him, you might turn him over to the police."

I shook my head. "I'm a lawyer, not an agent of the police. If I thought he killed Chris, I wouldn't take his case, but I wouldn't turn him over to the police, either. All I want is to talk to him. I want to know what happened to Chris."

After a moment, Bligh said, "I own a cabin in Arrowhead. We use it for shoots. Zack's up there. There's no phone, so you'll have to drive up."

"All right," I said. "How do I get there?"

Bligh called out, "Tommy, bring me a map to the cabin. And my checkbook, too." He looked at me. "I want to hire you to represent Zack."

"I told you, not if he killed Chris."

Tommy came into the room with the map and the checkbook. Bligh said, "He didn't. I'm sure of that."

"Why?"

"The judge was Zack's way out of this life," he said, his ironic gaze taking in the room, himself. "He grabbed at it with both hands and didn't look back."

"If that's true," I asked, "why are you so eager to help him now?"

"I want him back," Bligh said. His cold tone deflected pity, but for a second the guard went out of his eyes, and he looked old and sad.

Behind him, Tommy Callen's face closed like a fist.

Back in my car, I studied the map Bligh had given me and estimated that it would take four hours to reach the cabin. It was just after noon. I had no way of knowing how late I would be, so I went to see Josh before I left.

Driving to the hospital, I mulled over my conversation with Sam Bligh. His body seemed a metaphor of his character; powerful but crippled. He was shrewd and unsentimental and, despite his demurrers, probably capable of blackmail if it suited his purpose. It would've been easy to dismiss him as a exploiter, except that pornography was clearly more than just his business. I could see when he talked about the implicit violence of sex between men that it was something to which he'd given a lot of thought, but it wasn't an original thought. Depicting gay sex as a gladiator's contest was a way for some homosexual men to assure themselves of their masculinity, as if violence was the defining characteristic of manhood. I didn't buy it because I'd had the example of my father, a violent, brutal man, who choked on the fumes of his own rage like someone trapped in a burning building.

I wasn't sure that Bligh had completely convinced himself of it, either. He had felt something for Zack Bowen and it must have hurt when Zack rejected him for Chris. How much did it hurt, I wondered. How much had he wanted Zack back? Enough to kill? Not personally, not with his crippled legs, but he was a man of considerable resources. The more I looked into Chris Chandler's murder, the clearer it seemed that the least likely suspect was the one who was acting the guiltiest. Zack Bowen.

Josh was sitting up in his bed, with earphones plugged into his ears, eating a gray hospital lunch. When he saw me, he smiled happily and pulled out the earphones.

I kissed his cheek. "You look better today," I said.

"They're going to release me tomorrow afternoon. Will you give me a lift home?"

"Sure. I need to drive to Arrowhead, but I'll be back tonight."

He pushed his tray away. "This stuff is crap. Why are you going to the lake?"

I told him about Sam Bligh.

"This kid Zack must be something," he said.

"Catnip to older men, anyway."

He smiled. "Don't you fall for him."

"Not to worry," I answered. "Josh, I talked to Singh yesterday."

"I know," he said, mashing his food with his fork. "He told me this morning."

"Why don't you come and stay with me when they release you?"

"Not yet," he said, quietly. "I will, when it's time."

I didn't push it. "You want to talk about it?"

He looked at me tenderly. "I'm not afraid."

"No?"

He shook his head. "You remember that scene in *Indiana Jones and the Last Crusade*," he said, "where Jones is standing on the side of a canyon and he's got to get to the other side?"

"I didn't see that movie," I said.

"Well, he's searching for the Holy Grail, and he gets to this canyon and he has to cross to the other side, but all he can see is that if he does, he'll fall to the bottom. He's like terrified, but there's no going back. So he takes the leap. The leap of faith."

"And?"

"There's a bridge," Josh said, "but he couldn't see it because it was made out of exactly the same rock as the sides of the canyon and it blended in with them." He smiled. "That's what this feels like to me. I'm on one side and I have to get to the other, but I can't see how, so I just have to—" He broke off. "I lied to you, Henry. I am scared."

I crawled onto the bed and held him.

I was standing in the front of the elevators when I heard a woman say, "Hello, Mr. Rios."

"Detective McBeth," I said, turning toward her. She was in jeans and a UCLA sweatshirt. "What are you doing here?"

"I was visiting a friend," she replied, "and I thought I saw you walk by."

"You were visiting a friend on this floor?"

"Cops get AIDS, too," she said. "The person you were visiting—I hope it's not . . ."

"Yes," I said.

"I'm sorry. How's he doing?"

"They're releasing him tomorrow."

"That's good."

The elevator arrived and the door slid open. I started to board it when she touched my arm, lightly restraining me.

"If I could just have another minute of your time," she said.

I let the elevator go. "All right."

We moved away from the elevator, out of the hospital traffic. She said, "Mrs. Chandler called me this morning and told me that she and the judge separated a month ago because of his involvement with Zack Bowen. She also told me that the judge recently changed his will and made Zack Bowen a beneficiary."

"I know that," I said. "I told her to call you."

Her almond eyes registered surprise. "Did you? She didn't mention that. Are you representing the family?"

"I talked to her as a friend."

"I think you must know a lot more about all of this than you let on the last time I talked to you," she said. "I think you know where Zack Bowen is."

"Is he a suspect?"

"It's beginning to look that way," she said. "Look, if it makes any difference to you, I hope he's clean, but I can't rule him out until I talk to him."

"Why should you care whether he's clean?"

"Like I told you the last time, we have something in common. You and I, the judge, Zack Bowen."

"You keep implying you're gay," I said, "but you won't just come out and say it. That bothers me."

"Not everyone can be as open as you are," she said. "That doesn't mean we're not on the same team."

"I have to go now, Detective."

"Mr. Rios," she said, "you do know where he is. At least tell him he's better off talking to me than to someone else who might not understand his situation."

The elevator bell chimed and the doors opened. I got on it and left her there watching me.

It was getting toward dusk when I began my climb into the San Bernardino Mountains to Lake Arrowhead. I was so lost in my thoughts that I didn't see the red light in my rearview mirror until the sheriff was almost on top of me. I pulled into a turnaround, rolled down my window and waited.

The cop came over, leaned into my car and said, "Good evening, sir, may I see your license and your registration?"

Wordlessly, I handed them over.

He glanced at my license, then at me, and spent a moment longer on the registration. "You come up here often, Mr. Rios?"

"No," I said.

"You have to watch your speed on these mountain roads," he said, handing me back the papers. "I've been clocking you going five to ten miles over the posted limit. I think we can let it go this time, but I'd like you to be more careful."

"I will, Officer. Thank you."

He smiled. "You take care now."

I waited until he'd disappeared behind a bend before I started up again. The road flattened out and I was in a forest of tall pines. I kept the window down and felt the cool, pine-scented air on my face. I was thinking about leaps of faith. Life was full of them, though one seldom realized it except in retrospect. For me, coming out was a leap of faith, and then getting sober. Both events had changed my life in ways I could never have anticipated, but at the time it had seemed as if I hadn't had any choice in either matter. Now I knew better. The leap could be refused. Chris had refused it, but then had changed his mind. What was it? Zack? The onset of middle age? Some combination of the two? I wish he could have seen his way clear to talk to me. More than the mystery of his death, it was the mystery of Chris's life that had me out here on this unfamiliar road as darkness fell.

I came to the fork in the road described by the map Bligh had given me and went off to the right. Through a screen of trees, I could see the lake. Dusk had settled on the water like the wings of a enormous bird. The water lapped against the shore while the great, dark trees creaked overhead and a sliver of moon climbed the autumn sky. To my left, a clump of mailboxes marked the presence of houses. I slowed and looked for a private dock. When I found it, I turned off the road and headed up the hillside on a rutted, rocky path. I drove past a post with numbers on it and turned right until I came to a clearing, where I saw a car. I pulled up beside it, cut the motor and got out. It was so still I could hear the murmur of the water. From the edge of the clearing I saw Bligh's cabin. Yellow lights burned in the windows. I made my way down a rocky trail to the front door. Music played from within. I knocked at the door. The music stopped.

After a moment, the door opened and he stood behind the screen in a pair of sweatpants, his face and chest bathed in sweat.

"How did you find me?"

"Sam Bligh," I said. "Let me in, Zack. We have to talk."

13

HE STEPPED ASIDE TO LET ME PASS. I FOLLOWED HIM THROUGH A narrow kitchen gallery into a big square room with walls of rough-hewn wood and a stone fireplace, blackened with use, where a fire burned brightly. The room was furnished in chintz and wicker, bright rag rugs on the floor and geological survey maps on the wall. Against one wall was a rack containing a set of dumbbells. The twenty-five-pound weights were in the middle of the room; evidently I'd interrupted his workout. He picked up the weights and put them in their slots on the rack, then turned to face me. He was nervous but not exhausted and frightened, as he'd been when he came to my house. In the orange flicker of the firelight on his body, I saw him as if for the first time, drawn by the power of his extraordinary male beauty; the sinuous lines of his chest and ridged belly, the thick corded veins of his arms, the planes and hollows of his face, the long black hair, the startling blue eyes. He radiated pure sexual energy. It completely submerged his personality, leaving only his physical presence, like a blank screen for the projection of fantasy. Bligh's video, so preoccupied with the mechanics of sex, had completely missed the point of Zack's eroticism, but Bligh himself, apparently, had not, nor, I imagined, had Chris Chandler.

"I'm going to sit, do you mind?" I said, to break the silence.

He shook his head. "You want a beer or something?"

"No. We have a lot to talk about, Zack."

He sat down, cross-legged, on the floor, and waited.

"The police are looking for you," I said. "They found out that Chris changed his will to make you a beneficiary. Did you know that?"

"You mean, I would get something if he died?"

"That's right," I said. "Did you know he'd done that?"

A pause. "I didn't want him to," he said, "but he made such a big deal out of it. He said it was to show me that he was serious about us, when I asked him why we couldn't move in together after he moved out of his house."

"Do you know how much you were in the will for?"

"I didn't want to know," he said, a trace of anger in his voice. "I didn't want to think about him dying. I just wanted to be with him."

"You told me he didn't want to move in with you right away because he was concerned about his wife and his son."

"That's what he said," Zack replied.

"You didn't believe him?"

"Sometimes it seemed like he wasn't telling me everything," he said. He got up from the floor in a single fluid movement and went over to the fire and poked at it with an old rusted poker until it flared again. With his back to me, he said, "Chris had secrets."

"Like what?"

"Me," he said, turning, tapping his chest. "I was his secret from his wife, right? I figured he must have kept secrets from me, too."

"You think he was seeing someone else? You think that's why he didn't want to move in with you?"

"He told me I was imagining things," Zack said. "He said we could live together after he divorced her."

Bay hadn't mentioned anything about a divorce and I made a mental note to find out if he had started proceedings.

"Is that why you thought he wanted to see you the night he was killed, to tell you he was involved with someone else?"

He turned back to the fire and said, "I never believed he left her for me. I'm the kind of guy you keep around for a piece on the side. You don't marry me."

"Changing his will didn't convince you he was serious about you?"

"He could've changed it back."

"Bligh says the two of you were in love," I said.

He turned around and folded his arms across his chest. "Sam was jealous. He didn't know Chris."

"You were Bligh's lover before you met Chris."

"Sam got me off the streets," he said. "He helped me kick a speed habit. He gave me a place to live and got me a job at the restaurant. I owed him big time. I was ready to pay him back, any way he wanted."

"He wants you back," I said.

He snorted. "I think Miss Tommy might have something to say about that, but if that's what Sam wants, I guess I still owe him."

"What is it with you, Zack? Don't you have a life of your own, or is it just what other people want from you?"

"You remind me of Chris," he said in a hard voice. "You're smart. You're educated. You can just reach out and take what you want. The only thing I've ever been any good at is sex. Everyone wants to fuck me. It's been like that since I was a little sissy the other boys took around back for blow jobs. That's how I got things. That's how I still get them."

"What did you want from Chris?"

The hardness went out of his face. "Sam was half right. I was in love with Chris."

"Did you want him to take care of you?"

"No, I wanted to take care of him."

"How?"

"Sometimes, when we were alone, he cried," Zack said. "He just starting crying, and when I asked him why, he said it was because it was all so hard."

"What do you think he meant by that?"

"Keeping his secrets," he said. "Damn, it's tough being a fag. People hate you who don't even know you and the ones who know you, they're worse. Like his fucking son, what's his name, Joey. He got my number and called me and started screaming about how I stole his father. He said if I didn't let Chris come home, he was going to kill me."

"When did this happen?"

"I don't remember, but it was after Chris moved out, so it must have been a couple of weeks ago."

"Did you tell Chris?"

He nodded. "Yeah, I told him and he called Joey from my house and yelled at him. I could hear Joey yelling back at him, calling us cocksuckers and saying he hoped we got AIDS. That really pissed Chris off. He said he was sorry he had a son."

"Then what happened?"

"His wife got on the phone and he asked me to leave so he could talk to her. Afterwards, he came and found me and we went at it like he never had sex before."

"Zack, do you remember telling me that when you left Chris's chambers the night he was killed, you left the obelisk there?"

He looked at me blankly. "The what?"

"The pyramid, the thing that was used to kill him. You said you left it there."

He nodded. "Yeah," he whispered. "The sharp end was stuck in his neck, here." He touched the base of his neck. "I took it out and left it on his desk."

"You're sure about that?"

"I'm positive."

"But I told you on the phone, it wasn't there the next day when the police found him."

He shook his head. "I know you said that. But I left it, I swear I did."

"With your fingerprints on it?"

He stepped back as if I'd taken a swing at him. "I didn't think about that."

"If you handled it, your prints would have been on it. Are you sure you didn't take it?"

"I wasn't thinking about my fingerprints," he protested. "I just wanted to get out of there before someone came."

"Well, someone took it," I said, "and if you left it there, that can only mean someone came in after you left. Did you see anyone else around the court?"

He thought about it and shook his head.

"Think about it," I said. "From the moment you parked your car to the moment you drove out of the garage, did you see anyone at all?"

"Well, yeah, when I was leaving the garage. I almost had a crash."

"What happened?"

"I was so scared I went out the wrong way and I almost hit some guy, but he saw me and backed up so I could get out."

"Did you see him?"

"His lights were in my face."

"What about the car? You must have seen it when you drove past it."

"I don't remember," he said. "No, wait." He closed his eyes. "It was a big car, a four-wheeler."

"What color was it?"

"I didn't see the color, but it was dark."

Immediately, I thought of Joey Chandler's black Jeep Explorer. "Would you recognize it if you saw it again?"

"Maybe, I only saw it for a second."

"And the driver was male? Are you sure of that?"

He thought about it. "No, I didn't see his face, just a shape. Big shoulders, so I figured it was a guy."

"Old? Young? Tall? Short?"

"He was sitting down," he said. "Let me sleep on it. Maybe it'll come back to me."

I could hear the fatigue in his voice, so I let it go for now. A dark, four-wheel-drive vehicle. A driver with big shoulders. It wasn't much, but it could've been Joey. I didn't say anything to him, because I didn't want to taint his recollection before I could prod him for more details.

"This is what we have to do, Zack," I said. "We have to go back to L.A. and tell the police everything you've told me before they start concentrating on you as their main suspect."

"What if they arrest me?"

"They don't have sufficient evidence to arrest you. All they know is that Chris left his wife for you and put you in his will. They can't place you in the courtroom unless you tell them, or they find the murder weapon with your prints on it. But assuming that the murderer came back and took the obelisk, it's unlikely they're going to find it unless they also find him. Either way you're in the clear."

"I shouldn't tell them I found Chris?"

"If they had anything that put you in the room around the time he was killed, there would already be a warrant out for your arrest."

"Won't they find my fingerprints on the door or the desk or something?"

"That only proves you were in the room at some point and you told me you visited him occasionally."

He nodded. "Yeah, I did."

"Anyway, if the killer took the trouble to go back for the obelisk, he probably also remembered to wipe the doorknob and any other surface where he might have left prints."

"That makes sense," Zack said. "So what am I going to tell the police?"

"We'll work on that on the drive back into town."

The fire was almost out. He switched on a lamp and grabbed a sweatshirt from the floor and pulled it on.

"I'm beat, Mr. Rios," he said. "I can't talk to the cops like this. I'll be better in the morning."

I saw his point. Talking to the cops was going to be tricky, and I needed him to be rested and alert. A long drive in the middle of the night would only fatigue him further. On the other hand, he'd skipped on me before and I had my doubts about leaving him here alone. I told him so.

"Then you stay here, too," he said. "The sofa folds out." He smiled. "I'll give you my car keys."

"Keep them," I said. "All right, we'll drive into town first thing in the morning."

"Listen," he said. "I'm starving. Why don't you relax and I'll make something to eat?"

•   •   •

We ate scrambled eggs and bacon, played cards and then around midnight he made up the couch for me and went into his bedroom. I undressed and got into bed. I couldn't sleep. I'd told Bligh I wouldn't represent Zack if I believed he'd killed Chris, so I had to ask myself what I thought. The answer was, there was still a sliver of doubt in my mind about his innocence. I couldn't explain why, except that for it to have been someone else required some fancy moves; the murderer would have to have killed Chris, left before Zack arrived, and then returned after he left and gone undetected both times. In my experience, killing was rarely that complicated. On the other hand, after twenty years of listening to alibis, I had an acute sense of when I was being lied to, and either Zack was the best liar I had ever encountered or he was telling me the truth. I doubted it was the former. There were also better suspects than Zack; Joey Chandler, even Bligh. Had it been Joey whom Zack had seen driving into the garage? What about Bligh? Someone who lived right on the fine line of legality probably had as many friends who fell on one side of it as the other. I let it go. The police could figure out who killed Chris, that was their job. My concern was to clear Zack and then walk away from this case before it got any uglier.

At some point, I dropped off. A little later on, I awoke with a start to find Zack pressed up against me, his hand cupping my genitals.

"What do you think you're doing, Zack?" I said, rolling away from him and sitting up.

"Don't you want to?"

"I don't have sex with my clients."

"I'm not going to tell anyone."

"That's not the point. Go back to bed, all right, and we'll forget about this."

"I want to pay you for helping me," he said.

I laughed. "And here I thought it was because I was irresistible. Don't worry about my fee. Bligh offered to pay it."

"I don't want to take anything else from Sam," he said.

"That's fine," I said. "You and I can work it out later. Right now I want to get back to sleep. You should, too. We're going to have a long day tomorrow."

He got out of the bed and said, "Most guys don't turn me down." Before I could answer, he kissed me and said, "Thanks."

"Any time," I muttered, as he trotted off back to his room.

The sheets smelled of him. It took me a while to get back to sleep.

14

WHEN I WOKE UP THE NEXT MORNING, IT TOOK ME A MOMENT TO remember where I was. The cabin was bright but chilly and the only sound was the sweep of the wind through the trees. I sat up, yawned and checked my watch; it was a little after seven. We could make it back to the city by noon if we started now. I got out of bed, pulled on my clothes and went to wake Zack. A thin, shrill noise sounded from far off. I knocked at Zack's door. The noise became louder and I recognized it as a siren. Zack stumbled to the door, wiping the sleep from his eyes.

"What's that noise?" he asked.

"It sounds like a siren," I said. "Get dressed."

He didn't move, because now the siren was at the bottom of the road. Then, abruptly, it stopped, and cars began to rumble up the hill toward us.

"What's going on?" he asked.

"I don't know," I said. "Get some clothes on."

I went into the kitchen and looked out the window to the clearing where our cars were parked. I saw the flash of black and white as two patrol cars pulled in beside them, and then I heard the crackle of police radios carried through the still air.

"Shit," I said. "Zack, get out here, quick."

He came into the kitchen tucking his shirt into the pants. A couple of sheriffs were making their way down the path toward the cabin. Behind them I saw Yolanda McBeth.

"That's the homicide detective investigating Chris's murder," I said, pointing her out. "You don't talk to her."

"How did they know I was here?"

"I don't know," I said. "Maybe Bligh."

"He wouldn't tell them."

One of the sheriffs pounded the door and called, "Police."

"Stand back," I told Zack, as I unlocked the door and pulled it open.

"Zack Bowen?" the sheriff asked.

"No," McBeth said, squeezing past the two uniformed officers. "That's not him. Hello, Mr. Rios."

"Hello, Detective. What's up?"

"I have an arrest warrant for Zack Bowen," she said, removing a paper from the pocket of her heavy LAPD jacket. "For the murder of Chris Chandler."

I glanced at the warrant. "On what evidence?"

"We found the murder weapon in his apartment, along with some bloody clothing."

"You searched his apartment? When?"

"Late yesterday afternoon," she said. "Pursuant to a warrant. I'm sure the D.A. will provide you with a copy. Is Mr. Bowen here?"

"Just a minute, Detective. What exactly did you find at his apartment?"

She smiled indulgently. "We found a marble obelisk about a foot high that was given to the judge as an award by a lawyer's group." Her smile faded. "There are blood traces on it that match Judge Chandler's blood type. So does the blood on the clothes. Also, there was a partial thumb print on the obelisk. Bowen's. Is he here?"

"Zack," I said, nodding him over.

He looked wildly between me and McBeth, and I could see he was about to bolt, so I reached out and grabbed his arm.

"I didn't—" he started to say.

"Quiet," I said. "Everything will be fine."

The tension went out of his body. I tugged him over to McBeth.

"Zack Bowen, you're under arrest for the murder of Chris Chandler," she said, and read him his Miranda rights. When she finished, she asked, "Do you understand the rights I've just read to you?"

"Yes," he said quietly.

"Do you have anything to say?"

"No," I said. "He doesn't and no one is to speak to him about the case unless I'm present."

"Deputy," McBeth said to one of the sheriffs. "Take him up to the cars."

"Where's he going?" I asked her.

"We'll book him in San Bernardino and take him back to L.A. later on today. He'll be at County by tonight."

As one of the deputies handcuffed him, I said, "Remember, Zack, you don't talk to anyone unless I'm with you. I'll see you back in L.A."

Dazed, he let the sheriffs lead him up the path to their cars. McBeth said, "I'd like to search the cabin."

"Not without a warrant," I said.

"I don't need one," she replied. "The search is incident to an arrest."

"Nice try," I said, "but we both know that's bullshit."

"You shouldn't object if you don't have anything to hide."

"Oh, please," I said. I stepped outside the cabin and closed the door behind me. "You work fast, Detective. Had you already executed the search warrant when you talked to me at the hospital yesterday? Was that why you were so eager for me to tell you where Zack was?"

"You knew where he was," she said, starting up the trail to the clearing. I fell in step beside her.

"The question is, how did you find out?"

"You have other things to worry about than how I do my job," she replied, as we reached the clearing. "By the way, I will get a search warrant for the cabin."

"I give you my word as an officer of the court that I won't remove anything."

A caustic smile flickered across her face. "All the same, I'm going to leave one of the deputies here until I get back."

Zack was in the back seat of one of the patrol cars. He was crying, the tears running noiselessly down his face. An hour earlier I'd believed him innocent of Chris's murder, but now the evidence seemed inescapable. The deal I'd made with myself was that I wouldn't represent Chris's killer, and yet I was already thinking ahead to Zack's defense. I wasn't convinced of his guilt, and although I couldn't identify the source of my doubts, I trusted them. There was just something too pat about this solution, and the one thing I was certain of was that in things pertaining to Chris Chandler nothing was as it appeared.

I went over to the car and tapped at the window. Zack looked up me with his tear-stained face and managed to roll the window down a bit.

"Here," I said, handing him my handkerchief. He wiped his face with it.

"Mr. Rios," he said. "I swear I didn't do it."

"We're going to be spending a lot of time together, Zack," I said. "You better start calling me Henry."

When the patrol cars drove off, I noticed the driver of the second one, the one in which McBeth rode, was the same officer who had stopped me the day before for speeding. Kind of a coincidence. I thought about running into McBeth at the hospital. That was a coincidence, too. They seemed to have a way of happening between us.

I bickered about search and seizure law with the deputy whom McBeth had left to secure the cabin until he agreed to let me inside for five minutes to get the rest of my things. Once in, I looked through the bedroom Zack had occupied, but found nothing incriminating. Then I left and drove to a gas station, where I made a couple calls, to Josh, to let him know where I was, and to my investigator, Freeman Vidor, to set up a meeting. When I got back to L.A., my first stop was to see Sam Bligh.

Tommy Callen let me in, wearing even less than he had the day before, a black Speedo. His multihued hair was plastered to his head, giving him an even gaunter look. I again noticed the strange contrast between his young body and wasted, half-handsome face, and wondered if Bligh knew he was a speed freak.

Bligh was in the pool, swimming laps. He dragged himself through the water with short, powerful strokes, pulling his withered legs behind him. When he finished, he clung to the railing at the shallow end while Tommy lowered a wheelchair into the pool on a ramp, settled him in it, and then wheeled him out. Bligh's chest and belly were covered with a mat of white hair, but he was solid beneath it and his arms were thickly muscled. Tommy helped him with a robe, then he wheeled himself to a patio table set for two.

"Set another place for lunch," Bligh told Tommy. To me he said, "Find Zack?"

"I wasn't the only one," I replied. "The police arrested him this morning for Chris Chandler's murder."

Tommy drawled a slow, "Wow."

"Lunch," Bligh said sharply.

When he disappeared into the house, I said, "It's none of my business, but Tommy has the look of a speed freak to me."

"You're right," Bligh said. "It isn't any of your business. I want to hear about Zack."

I described the events of the morning and asked him, "Who knew that Zack was at your cabin?"

"No one," he said. "That was the point."

"Could Tommy have told someone?"

"Tommy didn't know. No one knew but me, until I told you. Why does it matter?" he added irritably. "We've got more serious problems to think about."

"Yes," I agreed. "Like the police finding the obelisk at Zack's apartment."

"You can't be sure it's the same one."

"McBeth's description matched Zack's," I replied. "Listen, Mr. Bligh, I'm willing to take Zack's case, but I don't want to be a patsy. Did Zack kill Chris Chandler?"

He fixed me with his fierce, cold eyes and said, "Zack's no more capable of murder than you are."

"Of course, you're prejudiced," I said, "because you're in love with him."

He grimaced. "I didn't say I was in love with him, I just said I wanted him back."

"I would imagine in your case it amounts to the same thing."

"Zack didn't kill anyone," he said, letting my comment pass. "If he did, he would've told me because he knows I'll protect him."

"Chris put Zack in his will," I said.

"Is that supposed to be a motive? Zack doesn't care about money."

"He thought Chris was seeing someone else."

Bligh shrugged. "So?"

"I don't think Zack's attitude about being cheated on is as casual as yours."

Bligh laughed a rumbling laugh. "If jealously's the motive, I'm a better suspect than Zack is."

"The thought did cross my mind," I said.

"Pretty hard for a cripple to bang someone over the head."

"Maybe someone did it for you."

He laughed again. "Who? Tommy? In between fixes? Don't be stupid, Mr. Rios. My vanity was wounded when Zack left me for Chandler, but I got over it."

Tommy appeared pushing a trolley laden with food. I took it as my cue to leave.

"Leaving?" Bligh asked.

"I have errands," I said.

"You wouldn't take my money yesterday. Will you take it now?"

"Zack won't take it," I said. "He's the client."

"I see," Bligh said, smiling bleakly. "Tell me something, do you think a jury would send a cripple to the gas chamber?"

Tommy dropped a glass.

I was almost out the gate when I heard Tommy Callen calling me. I turned around. He came running down the driveway.

"I have to tell you something," he said, out of breath.

"What is it?"

"I saw Zack the night the guy was killed. The judge."

"Where?"

"At the restaurant. Azul?" He mispronounced it. "I ate dinner there that night with some friends. Zack waited on us. After he got off work, he came into the bar and had a drink with us before we all split up."

"What time was that?"

"I don't remember, but I was back here by twelve, so it had to be before then."

"Okay," I said. "I knew Zack was working at the restaurant that night, so I'm not sure why you're telling me this."

"Because of Sam," he said. "Sam can't get around unless I drive him. He didn't go anywhere that night because I was at the restaurant. Ask Zack."

"Oh," I said, understanding. Tommy hadn't meant to alibi Zack, he was trying to protect Bligh. Was he really so stupid to think Bligh was serious about taking the rap for Chris's murder?

"Okay?" Tommy said.

"Sam was here," I said. "What about Zack? Did he tell you he was going to see Chris?"

He shook his head. "He had a drink with us and then he left."

"Did he seem upset?"

"Zack's a quiet one," he replied.

"I got the impression that you and Zack don't get along," I said.

"Zack never hurt me," he drawled, "but he sure did a number on Sam."

"Sam says he's over it. Is he?"

"Whatever Sam says," he answered. "When you see Zack, tell him I said hello."

15

From Bligh's house, I went to the hospital, where Josh was waiting for me to drive him home. First, though, I stopped at the nurse's station on the fourth floor to play a hunch.

"Excuse me," I said to the sandy-haired male nurse behind the counter, "I'm looking for someone."

He smiled and said, "Aren't we all? Does yours have a name?"

I smiled, and wondered if he just assumed every unattached male who wandered into the AIDS ward was gay.

"I don't know his name. All I know is that he's a police officer and he was still here as of yesterday."

"Lily Law? Here? I don't think so."

"He had a visitor yesterday afternoon around this time," I said. "A very pretty black woman."

"Her I remember," he said. "She was wandering the halls like the angel of death. I asked her if I could help her and she was quite snippy. She said she was waiting for someone, but I heard the fuck-off in her voice." He studied me. "In fact, didn't I see you talking to her?"

"Yeah," I said. "You're sure she wasn't here to visit a patient?"

"Well, if she was, I hope she didn't find him."

"Thanks," I said.

Josh was sitting in a chair in his room leafing through a magazine. I stood at the doorway and watched him. He wore baggy jeans and a white cotton cable-knit sweater that enclosed him in its bulk and made him seem thinner than ever. His skull was clearly visible in his face. It gave him an agelessness that made it hard to remember he was only twenty-nine years old. He flipped the pages of the magazine slowly, as if with effort. He sighed.

"Josh?"

He smiled at me. "Hey, here's my boyfriend."

"Ready to go home?"

He rose from the chair stiffly, the neuropathy slowing his movements, and grabbed his red backpack. "All set."

"No box of medicines this time?"

"Not this time," he said, taking my arm. "Buy me some ice cream. I've been wanting it all day."

Of course, no one actually sold ice cream west of La Brea, not in the realm of the physically fit, so we ended up at a frozen yogurt stand on Santa Monica. He stood at the counter, sarcastically reading the minuscule calories per ounce of the ices, fat-free yogurts and tofuttis, while the puzzled counterboy waited for him to make his selection.

"When did they outlaw milk fat?" Josh demanded.

"Beg pardon?" the boy said.

"Don't torment him, Josh. It's not his fault."

"I want a sundae with cappuccino yogurt and extra nuts," Josh said.

"The fat-free fudge?" the boy asked.

Josh said, "Oy vey iz meir," in perfect imitation of his father.

We sat on the sidewalk at a white plastic table beneath a pink awning, watching the late-afternoon traffic clog the boulevard. One of the big gyms was across the street, occupying nearly the entire block, and men in Lycra shorts and spaghetti-strap tank tops, hauling huge gym bags, darted among the cars on their way to cardio-funk class.

"What can those guys be carrying that requires such big bags?" I asked Josh.

"Moisturizers," he replied. He pointed out a pumped-up boy waiting at the corner for the light to change and said, "Remember when I had a body like that?"

"You taught me the names of the muscle groups. I think my favorite was latissimus dorsi. It sounded like the title of a papal encyclical."

"It seems silly now that I cared about all that," he said, spooning melted frozen yogurt and non-fat-free fudge into his mouth. "But most things people care about are silly. They don't think about the ones that matter."

"Such as?"

"Getting from one breath to the next one. So what happened this morning up in Arrowhead? Did the cops break down the door?"

After I described Zack's arrest, I said, "McBeth didn't try to talk to you yesterday after I left, did she?"

"Remind me who she is."

"The homicide detective. Good-looking black woman. I think she tailed me to the hospital yesterday when I came to see you."

"Why?" he asked, dipping into the last of his sundae.

"Because she was hoping I would lead her to Zack Bowen," I said. "Instead, she followed me upstairs and waited for me, then claimed she'd been visiting a friend with AIDS and implied she was a dyke."

"And she's not?"

I shook my head. "What she is, is smart. She caught me at a moment when she knew my guard would be down and tried to establish some kind of connection to get me to tell her where Zack was. When I wouldn't tell her, she had me followed up to Arrowhead."

"Isn't that illegal?"

"No. Duplicitous, but not illegal. It makes me wonder if she's shaved some other edges in her investigation of Chris's murder."

Josh walked into his apartment, went into the bathroom and threw up. He emerged, wiping his mouth on a washcloth.

"Food never tastes as good coming up as it did going down," he said.

"What happened?"

"Just a touch of AIDS," he said, glancing at his answering machine. "Seven messages. That's all my living friends. Present company excluded."

"I need to call the jail to see if Zack's there yet." I called and was told he had arrived an hour earlier, so I made arrangements to see him. When I finished, I handed the phone to Josh, who'd been writing down his messages. "I'm going down to see Zack, but I'll be back after that."

"You don't have to," he said. He touched the catheter in his chest. "I'll just be here infusing chemical substances."

"What if I want to?"

"Then you can bring a video. I'm in the mood for bad Bette Davis."

"As if there's any other kind," I said.

An hour later, I was sitting in an attorney room at the county jail waiting for Zack, with a fresh pad of paper on the table before me. Through the supposedly soundproof walls I heard the endless clatter of the place, shouts and groans, cell doors being opened and slammed shut, trolleys being rolled down the fetid halls, heavy footsteps, jangling keys and someone whistling "Danny Boy." The air was thick with the musk of confined and violent men, jailers and inmates alike, an incendiary combination of rage and fear and suffering. Some day a spark would set it off and the explosion would leave the equivalent of a black hole in the moral universe that decreed such places should exist.

A deputy sheriff pulled the door open and brought Zack into the room. He was in an orange jumpsuit, the laces removed from his shoes. He was glad to see me in a way that suggested he hadn't been sure he ever would again. The deputy sat him down across the table from me and removed his cuffs, then went outside.

He wiped his nose on his sleeve, and in that gesture I saw the street kid he'd once been. It was in his expression, too, a look of defiance that didn't quite mask the terror in his eyes.

"Where have they got you?" I asked him.

"In with the other queens," he said, understanding me. "It's not so bad."

"I'd rather they kept you out of the general population."

"I can take care of myself," he said.

"But you don't have to," I reminded him. "You've got me and I'm going to tell you something, Zack. Chris was my friend, but I'll try to help you, even if you killed him."

"I didn't," he said, without emphasis.

"Then how did the obelisk get into your apartment?"

"I don't know," he said, frustration in his voice. "I've been thinking about it all day, and I can't figure it out."

"Listen, Zack. Sometimes people do things in a blackout and then don't remember doing them afterwards. Could that have happened to you? Were you angry at Chris? Were you drunk or on drugs?"

"No, no, no," he said. "I remember everything." He squeezed the edge of the table until his knuckles went white. "I wish I could forget how he looked, with his face in a puddle of blood and his brains coming out of the back of his head. Do you think I could do something like that?"

"When was the last time you were in your apartment?"

"Right after it happened," he said. "My clothes were bloody, so I went home to change. That's when I decided to find you and then we had the earthquake."

"What happened when the earthquake hit? Didn't the building across the street from yours collapse?"

He nodded. "It was crazy. Things falling, breaking, people screaming, then this big noise outside like an explosion. I went out to the street and that building was like a stack of pancakes the way the floors fell. I helped get people out until the cops came and then they evacuated us. After that, I drove to your house."

"You haven't been back to your apartment since?"

"From your place I went to Sam's, then up to Arrowhead."

"So it's been four days since you were home?"

"Yeah," he said, "less than a week. It feels like forever."

"Did anyone else besides you have a key to your apartment?"

"Yeah, the manager, I guess, Karen. And Chris. I gave Sam a key, but he gave it back to me."

"Why Sam?"

"I let him use my place to shoot a scene for one of his movies."

"You do remember leaving the bloody clothes in your apartment, right?"

He nodded. "Yeah, I threw them into the closet and then took a shower. He was cold."

"What?"

"Chris was cold," he said. "I turned him over and wiped his face with my sleeve and then I lay down on top of him and held on to him." He blinked hard, as if to clear away the memory. "That's how I got blood on my clothes."

"When you picked up the obelisk, how did you handle it? What part did you pick up?"

"I don't remember."

"It could be important, Zack. Every detail could be important."

"I don't want to think about it now."

"All right, but later I'd like you to write down everything you remember."

He nodded. "It's been a long time since I was in jail," he said, with a trace of a smile. "I forget what happens now."

"The D.A. has seventy-two hours to arraign you or release you. I wouldn't count on being released. At the arraignment, you'll plead not guilty and I'll get copies of the police report, the search warrant and whatever else they have at this point. By law, you have to be tried within sixty days, but we'll continue the case until we're ready to go to trial."

He'd been following closely and now he said, "No."

"No what?"

"I don't want to continue the case. I want it over with as soon as possible."

"Zack, I have no idea yet how much investigation this is going to require."

"But I didn't kill Chris," he said. "Can't I just say that? Don't you believe me?"

"The obelisk," I said.

"I can't explain that."

"Unless we can, we're dead."

"Someone put it there," he said.

"You mentioned the manager of your building, Karen? What's her last name?"

"Holman," he said, and spelled it for me. "What are you going to do, Henry?"

"Drive out to your building and take a look. Maybe someone saw something." I glanced at my notes. "Chris was the only person who had a key to your place, other than the manager?"

"Yeah."

"Do you know if he kept it on him?"

"I guess it was on his key chain."

I made a note to find out about the disposition of Chris's property.

"And Bligh had a copy but he returned it to you, and you're sure of that?"

"I remember he gave it back to me."

I got up. "I guess that's it for now. I'll give you a call tomorrow. Is there anything you need?"

"I—nothing. Thank you. That's all."

16

I SPENT THE NIGHT AT JOSH'S APARTMENT. WE WATCHED *BEYOND the Forest*, the Bette Davis movie where she delivers the line "What a dump," beloved of drag queens everywhere. We ate Chinese food and he managed to keep his down. I managed to put Zack Bowen and Chris Chandler out of my mind for a few hours. The next morning, however, I checked my messages and found half a dozen calls from local media types who had learned I was representing Zack and had started to sniff out the tabloid possibilities of Chris's murder. I didn't return any of their calls, but I did phone the D.A.'s office and a deputy D.A. confirmed that a murder charge was being filed against Zack and arraignment was set for the next day. Then I drove back to the valley, to Zack's apartment, to see what I could see.

It was a balmy autumn morning. The air was clear and visibility was good, so there was no relief at all from the seediness of Zack's neigh borhood. Both sides of the street were lined with apartment buildings put up in the 60s and apparently untouched since then. Their Disney land pastels had long since faded to a dirty whitewash, torn awnings flapped in the breeze, the front yards were forests of overgrown banana trees and jade plants. The earthquake had accelerated the ruin, cracking walls and blowing out windows, and there, across the street from Zack's building, behind a recently installed cyclone fence, was what the media called The House of Death.

The three stories had collapsed, one atop the other, into the subterranean garage, and twenty-seven people were killed. It didn't look particularly lethal now, just a hulking mass of rubble. Flowers and messages had been stuck into the fence and there was a row of burned-out candles in front of it. I doubted that anyone would make a TV movie out of this disaster; the neighborhood was not photogenic, the people who lived in it were poor. But as a metaphor for the city, it had a certain chilling aptness.

There was yellow police ribbon strung across the entrance to Zack's building. I ducked beneath it and found myself in a rectangular court-yard paved with concrete. It was bare of adornment except for a few potted plants and a half-dozen patio chairs and a couple of plastic patio tables. The building was two stories high. Along the second floor was a wooden railing. The front doors of the apartments opened onto the patio and I surmised from their numbering that Zack's apartment, 206, was on the second floor. The place appeared to be completely de-serted. I was wondering about my next step when I heard the distinc-tive click of a safety being released at my back.

"Put your hands on your head and turn around. Slow."

I complied. A thin, pale woman in a blue sundress stood a few feet away from me, pointing a .38 caliber handgun at my chest.

"Karen Holman?" I ventured.

"How do you know my name?"

"My name is Henry Rios. I'm a lawyer for one of your tenants, Zack Bowen."

"You don't look like a lawyer," she said, indicating my jeans and tee shirt, which was what I usually wore when I wasn't going to court or meeting a client.

"I have a business card in my wallet," I said. "That's in my back pocket. I'll have to—"

"Don't move," she said. "Teddy, come out here."

A tow-headed boy of nine or ten emerged from behind a door marked "Manager" and came to her side.

"Go get the man's wallet," she said. "It's in his back pocket."

The boy smirked and darted behind me. I felt quick, small fingers lift the wallet from my pocket and then he ran back to the woman.

"Find his business card," she said.

The boy thumbed through my wallet, scattering credit card receipts and other bits of paper on the ground until he found my cards and handed one to the woman.

"Like this?" he asked.

She took it from him, glanced at it and then lowered the gun, setting the safety as she did. The boy, I noticed out of the corner of my eye, was surreptitiously pocketing a five he'd lifted from my wallet.

"We've had looters," she said, by way of apology. "Give him his wallet back."

Teddy tossed me my wallet. I caught it and stuck it in my pocket.

"Are you the only ones here?" I asked her.

"Yeah, since the quake," she said. "It cracked the foundation and the city ordered everyone out. I stayed behind to keep an eye on the place until the owners decide what to do."

"Where are the rest of the tenants?"

"They scattered," she said.

"Did you know Zack's in jail for murder?" I asked her.

She nodded. "The police came day before yesterday and searched his apartment. The woman who was in charge, black girl, kind of rude, she told me about Zack."

"Did you know Chris Chandler?"

"Zack's boyfriend? Only to say hi. I don't believe it about Zack."

"Why?"

She pushed her fingers through her lank hair. "Zack's the nicest guy you'd ever want to meet. Everyone thought so."

"Can I take a look at his place?"

"Well," she said, hesitantly, "I don't want any problems with the police."

"There won't be," I said. "As his lawyer, I have the same rights as the police to look at his apartment."

"Will it help him?"

"Could be," I said.

"All right," she said, decisively. "Teddy, go get me the keys."

While we waited for Teddy, I asked her, "Have you been here the whole time since the quake?"

She shook her head. "They evacuated everyone. We just came back two days ago, same day that the cops showed up. I thought they had come to throw us out. I guess we really shouldn't be here, but it's better than sleeping in a tent in the park."

I calculated. "So as far as you know, the building was deserted for what, a couple of days?"

"A couple of days after the quake, they let the tenants come in for fifteen minutes to take what they could, but other than that, there hasn't been anyone here."

Teddy came out of their apartment with a ring of keys and gave them to her.

"What did you think about camping out in the park?" I asked him.

"It was boring," he replied, exaggerating the word in the manner of sitcom characters.

It was hard to tell in Zack's apartment what damage had been done by the quake and what damage had been done by the cops, but between the two forces, the place was pretty torn up. There wasn't much to it, a small living room separated from the kitchen by a breakfast counter and a slightly larger bedroom and bath at the end of a hall. Even in the disarray there was evidence that it had been fixed up lovingly at one time. The bedroom walls were pale green and the striped curtains matched the bedspread. The bedboards had been stripped to their original pine and lightly whitewashed. Against the wall was an armoire, also pine, that housed a TV and a VCR. The cops had emptied the closet, scattering clothes and shoes.

The living room was decorated with a suite of wicker furniture, the cushions tossed to the floor and trampled. On the coffee table was the remains of a collection of turtles. There were turtles of all sizes, made from ceramic, metal, glass and wood. Why turtles, I wondered, picking up a small brass figurine. I tucked it into my pocket to take to him for his cell. To cheer him up.

In the kitchen, the shelves had been emptied and drawers opened and upturned on the counter. A work schedule was attached to the refrigerator door by a turtle magnet. According to the schedule, Zack had worked the dinner shift the night Chris was murdered. I took it off the refrigerator and folded it into my pocket, dropping the magnet. When I bent to pick it up, I saw the corner of a photograph sticking out from beneath the refrigerator. I retrieved it. It showed Chris with his arm around Zack, the two of them smiling. I put that in my pocket, too.

Karen Holman was waiting for me outside the apartment.

"Were you in the apartment when the police searched it?"

"No," she said. "I don't think they wanted me around."

"Really? Why did you think that?"

"The black lady told me to stay out of the way," she said. "So I let them in and waited out here."

"Did you see them take anything out?"

"They were coming and going for a good long while," she said. "It was kind of confusing."

"You said you knew Chris by sight," I said. "Was there ever any trouble between them? Fighting? Complaints from the neighbors?"

"No," she said. "Nothing like that."

"How long has he lived here?"

"Year and a half maybe. Zack's a sweetheart," she said. "He was usually home during the day, and if I had to work late he'd keep an eye on Teddy for me when he got home from school."

"What's going to happen to the building?"

"The owner's waiting on FEMA to see if the foundation can be fixed," she said. "Otherwise I guess they'll tear it down."

"Thanks for your time," I said.

"Sure," she said. "Anything I can do to help Zack, you just let me know."

"Why turtles?" I asked Zack the next morning in lockup, where he was waiting to be arraigned.

He put the little brass turtle in the palm of his hand and intoned, "Slow and steady wins the race."

"You mean Aesop's fable, the tortoise and the hare? You identify with the tortoise?"

He closed his hand on the turtle and grinned. "Stupid, huh?"

"I don't think so."

"Can I keep it?"

"That's why I brought it," I said. I took the picture of Chris and Zack from my coat pocket and gave it to him. "I thought you might want this, too."

He looked at it for a long time. "It's like it never really happened," he said, finally. "Me and Chris."

A few minutes later, Zack pled not guilty to the charge of murder in the first degree.

"How's two weeks from today for the prelim?" the judge, a youthful-looking Asian woman named Soo, asked me.

"That's fine with the defense," I replied. "I've exchanged discovery requests with the People. Would you set that as the compliance date, too?"

"You got it," she said. "Anything else?"

"I'd like to orally notice a fifteen-thirty-eight-point-five motion for the same day," I said. "We'll be challenging the sufficiency of the search warrant."

"Fine," she said. "Is that it?"

"Bail," I said. "We'd ask the court to set reasonable bail."

"People?" she asked the D.A.

"This case involves the murder of a judicial officer," he said. "People oppose bail."

"May I be heard?" I asked.

She shook her head impatiently. There were twenty cases behind us. "I'm going to deny bail without prejudice to your right to renew your request at the prelim. Which will be before Judge Torres-Jones." She handed the file to her clerk and took up the next one. "Thank you, gentlemen. Defendant is remanded. People versus Lawrence."

"I'll call you later," I told Zack, as the marshals stepped forward to return him to county jail.

"Don't forget," he replied, attempting a smile.

The D.A. gave me a copy of the information charging Zack and a stack of preliminary materials. They included the initial police report, the search warrant and the medical examiner's report. After I escaped the press, I went downstairs to the cafeteria to take a closer look at them. The cafeteria smelled of grease and coffee. The yellow walls tried for brightness, but suggested jaundice instead. A foursome of uniformed cops wolfed down plates of chorizo and eggs. I got a cup of coffee and found a corner table that looked out, through tinted glass, on Temple Street.

This was my dilemma; either Zack killed Chris Chandler and was lying to me about it or, contrary to the apparent evidence of Zack's guilt, someone else did. My intuition rejected Zack as the murderer, but I couldn't very well expect the jury to acquit him based on my word or his. So far, there was a handful of circumstances that could be developed into the classic defense known by the criminal law bar as ODDI; the other dude did it. When I narrowed the field of possible suspects, I came up with Joey Chandler.

I wasn't happy about it, but there it was. The troubled son, a raging little boy who'd grown into a sullen adolescent, about whom both his parents felt deeply guilty. It was mostly through Chris and Bay that I knew anything at all about Joey, and the one phrase I'd come to associate with him was "doing better," as in "Joey's doing better now that he" fill in the blank. Stopped wetting his bed, is in therapy, has taken up weight lifting. I doubted whether I had spoken to him more than a dozen times in his twenty years on earth. He was not the kind of child who took much interest in his parents' friends, nor, truthfully, was I the kind of friend who took much interest in my friends' children.

To judge by its messiness, the crime was one of anger rather than premeditation, and Joey had expressed his anger at Chris on several occasions both before and after the murder. Joey would also have known how to get in and out of the courthouse, and it would not have been unusual for him to visit his father there. He had known that the obelisk had been used to murder Chris before it was known by the police; though, admittedly, I was stretching things here since he hadn't actually responded to my question when I asked him about it. Zack had seen a man in a dark, four-wheel-drive vehicle entering the courthouse garage as he was leaving. Joey drove a black Jeep Grand Cherokee. If it was Joey, and he had removed the obelisk, could he have planted it in Zack's apartment? Chris had a key to the apartment which was, as yet, unaccounted for, and there was a five-day period when his apartment building had been empty. Finally, until I prompted her, Bay hadn't told the police that Chris had left her, thus deflecting suspicion away from Joey.

This last thought gave me the most qualms, because it implied knowledge by Bay. Knowledge of what? That her son had killed his father? Or something less clear, but equally damning; maybe that he couldn't account for his whereabouts the night Chris was killed or simply that he had expressed his hatred for Chris to her in a way that frightened her for him. Only she knew the answer to that, and once she learned that I was representing Zack, she wouldn't be telling me.

Of course, my entire theory of Joey's putative guilt was as flimsy as a house of cards. He had only to provide an alibi and I was back to square one and who did that leave? Bligh? That was even a further stretch. Who else? As Zack pointed out, Chris kept secrets. I knew that better than anyone. The problem was that he had taken his secrets to his grave.

17

I BEGAN WITH THE AUTOPSY REPORT. IT WAS HARD GOING BECAUSE I'd read a sentence, then remember it was Chris whose body was being dissected, and have to stop. I reminded myself that somewhere in the mass of clinical details I might find clues about how Chris had been killed that would help me prepare a defense. That made it easier, but I was glad the D.A. hadn't provided me with the medical examiner's pictures.

The M.E. had attributed the cause of death to multiple skull fractures to the back of Chris's head by a blunt object. The fractures had caused internal bleeding; his brain had been drowned in its own blood. There was an absence of defensive wounds or abrasions, suggesting he'd been taken by surprise by the first blow and either stunned or knocked unconscious. There was a bruise on the right side of his face, apparently caused when he fell to the floor, face down. The M.E. noted that the body had been found face up, suggesting that it had been moved post-mortem. That was Zack, turning Chris over. Time of death was estimated to be between 10:00 P.M. and midnight.

A toxicological analysis of Chris's blood revealed a blood alcohol level of .12, a reading that made him legally intoxicated. For someone of Chris's height and weight, that meant a lot of drinks consumed over a fairly short period of time. The medical examiner had also found partially digested food in his stomach, suggesting a recent meal.

A mental picture began to emerge of that night. Chris had gone to the court sometime in the evening, worked for a bit, and then gone out to dinner. Either before dinner or with dinner he'd had several drinks, enough to have felt his liquor. I had never known Chris to be a solitary drinker or much of a drinker at all, particularly after Bay stopped. It was hard for me to see him sitting alone in a restaurant going through a bottle of wine. I liked another explanation: that he'd met someone for dinner, someone whom he'd felt the need to face on a few drinks.

His killer had struck him from the back, taking Chris by surprise. The combination of the first blow and the liquor had stunned him because he hadn't put up a fight. His murderer had struck another half-dozen blows before he left. The killer was someone Chris knew and who had access to the courthouse. I had been assuming it was someone who had met Chris at the courthouse. Maybe, though, it was the same person with whom he'd had dinner, and then they'd gone back to the courthouse together. Someone, a guard, another judge working at the courthouse late, might have seen Chris going to dinner or returning. I made a note to follow up on that.

I set the coroner's report aside and flipped through the remaining reports until I found the search warrant that had authorized the search of Zack's apartment. Challenging the warrant would be my first line of defense because, if successful, I could exclude the obelisk and the bloody clothes and gut the prosecution's case. There would then be no trial and no pointing the finger of guilt at Joey Chandler.

I found the officer's affidavit, the document that was supposed to provide probable cause to the judge who issued the warrant. I scanned down to the signature line and was not surprised to see Yolanda Mc-Beth's name. I went back to the top of the page and began to read. Immediately, the words "anonymous citizen informant" jumped off the page.

"On October 12th, your affiant received a call from an anonymous citizen informant who resides in the same apartment complex as the suspect but who declined to further identify himself," she had written. "The informant told your affiant that on October 8 at approximately 1 o'clock in the morning he was sitting at his kitchen table in his apartment on the second floor of the building when he saw the suspect pass in front of his window. The informant said the suspect's shirt front was smeared with what appeared to be blood and he was clutching an object in his right hand described by the informant as made of stone. The informant said he could see clearly because of the overhead lighting in the hallway outside the window. The informant told your affiant that he went to the door of his apartment and opened it wide enough to have a view of the suspect entering his apartment. His observations at that time confirmed the bloodied shirt and stone object. The informant said that shortly after, there was a severe earthquake that caused considerable damage to the apartment complex and he, along with the other tenants, including the suspect, exited the complex to the street. The informant told your affiant that he observed the suspect had changed his shirt. The informant said he attempted to engage the suspect in conversation, but the suspect appeared nervous and, without reentering his apartment, got into his vehicle and left the area. The informant said that the tenants were subsequently evacuated from the building because of structural damage and have only been allowed to return for a few minutes to recover personal items. The informant told your affiant that he watched for the suspect but, that to his knowledge, the suspect did not return to the building. The informant said he subsequently learned of Judge Chandler's murder from the newspaper and recognized him from his picture as the man whom he had sometimes seen in the suspect's company in the past six months.

"The informant stated that he did not wish to identify himself because he feared for his personal safety should the suspect learn he had spoken to the police. Your affiant attempted to assure the informant he would be protected if he stepped forward, but the informant terminated the conversation at that point. Attempts to trace the call were unsuccessful. Your affiant has personally attempted to interview all the second-floor tenants of the building, but this task has been made impossible by the fact that the building has been evacuated and the former tenants have scattered, some of them remaining at temporary shelters while others have apparently left the area. None of the tenants whom your affiant has been able to interview have admitted to being the informant. The suspect has apparently fled the jurisdiction. It is your affiant's belief that the objects which the informant observed the suspect to have been in possession of the night of the murder, e.g., the bloodied clothing and the stone object, remain in the suspect's apartment."

I stopped reading, sipped my now-cold coffee and reviewed what I remembered about the legal status of searches conducted on the basis of anonymous tips. When I'd first started practicing law, the courts had been extremely suspicious of these kinds of searches because of the obvious danger that the police had simply manufactured the anonymous tips they were based on. As a result, the courts had adopted complicated rules that made anonymous tip warrants difficult to obtain. After a decade and a half of conservative Supreme Court majorities chipping away at the exclusionary rule, the old rigid standard to which this kind of search warrant would once have been subjected had been replaced by a sloppy "totality of the circumstances" test designed to give the cops plenty of leeway in justifying the search. Virtually all that survived of the old rules was the requirement that the police produce some independent corroborative evidence in support of the anonymous tip.

I returned to the affidavit in search of McBeth's corroboration. She'd confirmed that Zack was the lessee of the apartment she wanted to search, but that wasn't corroborative of what she expected to find in it. Apparently realizing this, she'd included a paragraph explaining why she believed Zack might be the killer, including, I noted, that "suspect had a homosexual relationship with the decedent." Zack was a queer, ergo, he was a murderer. For good measure, she mentioned that Zack was a beneficiary of Chris's will; he was not just a queer, but a greedy one.

She described Chris's head wounds and speculated that they were the result of his having been bludgeoned by the informant's stone object. She speculated further that the stone object was "an award decedent received from the county bar association. According to decedent's court clerk, the award was a marble obelisk that decedent kept on his desk and which was missing from the scene when his body was found." She also included her observation that, from the amount of blood at the crime scene, "it is likely the killer would have been blood-ied, explaining the blood the informant noticed on the suspect's shirt."

So there it was, her corroboration: blunt force head trauma, a homo-sexual relationship, a possible monetary motive, a missing award and a bloody death. Of themselves, those observations would never have jus-tified issuing a search warrant for Zack's apartment. As corroboration, they were still pretty thin. The missing obelisk, for instance. When had Chris's court clerk last seen it? How did the clerk know he hadn't taken it home sometime before the murder? How did McBeth know that what her informant had seen was the same object without a more detailed description either of the obelisk or the informant's stone ob-ject? What about color, size, dimensions, weight? Why hadn't she at-tempted to gather this information from whoever had given Chris the award? Why wasn't there anything about the kind of injury Chris had received to support her conclusion that the obelisk was a possible weapon? Wouldn't so bizarre a murder weapon have made distinctive wounds? Where was the medical examiner's affidavit? Why couldn't he have been struck by a club or a knife or even the ashtray he kept in his desk drawer?

Her conclusion about the blood on Zack's shirt could also be at-tacked. Wouldn't there have been a particular kind of splattering from the blows Chris received? Would there have been drops or puddles? Did either correspond to the blood on Zack's shirt that the informant had observed? Couldn't it have been Zack's own blood from a cut? Would it have been fresh or dried by the time the informant suppos-edly saw it?

The issuing judge had not asked himself these questions before he signed the warrant and now another judge would decide whether he should have. The biggest obstacle, however, was not the suffi-ciency of McBeth's warrant, but the fact that she had found the ob-elisk in Zack's apartment. The reviewing judge was not supposed to

take this into consideration. That judge was required to place herself in the position of the judge who issued the warrant and determine, *de novo,* whether the affidavit supplied probable cause. As a
practical matter, it would be hard for the judge to put out of her
mind that McBeth's anonymous tip had panned out. A lot would
ride on who the judge was. The preliminary hearing would take
place in the municipal court before a judge named Torres-Jones,
about whom I knew nothing. I could bring the suppression motion
as part of the prelim or wait until we reached Superior Court for
trial. I tucked my papers into my briefcase and went off to the
county law library on First Street to research Torres-Jones.

She'd been on the municipal court for fifteen years. She was one of a
number of muni court judges who'd been appointed by the last
Democratic governor, a liberal, and then languished there through
the administrations of his right-wing Republican successors. The
Republicans appointed ex-District Attorneys while Torres-Jones, in addition to being a Democrat, was a former Public Defender. Ex-P.D.s
were thought to be unreliable on law-and-order issues but more often
than not, once they became judges, they earned reputations as harsh
sentencers. The reason was that they'd heard all the bullshit from
criminal defendants when they represented them and were less likely
to be swayed by it on the bench. Torres-Jones had such a reputation,
but she was also known for being tough on cops. On the other hand,
her most recent judicial profile mentioned that she planned to run for
the Superior Court next time there was a vacant seat. These days,
judicial candidates liked to have police endorsements to assure the
paranoid public that they were on the right side of the law. This was
going to be a high-profile case and she might not want to be the judge
who suppressed crucial evidence. That, of course, would be true of any
judge who heard the suppression motion, since they all had to stand
for reelection sooner or later.

I studied the headshot that accompanied her profile. She had a
pleasant, plump face framed by a mass of dark hair threaded with gray.

She was fifty-three years old. As a lawyer she'd been active in the women's and Latino bar associations and as a judge she'd served on the state bar's commission on gender equality and served two terms as presiding judge of the municipal court. A good old-fashioned liberal; no wonder her career was stalled. I decided to set the suppression hearing before her.

18

THE NEXT DAY I MET WITH MY INVESTIGATOR, FREEMAN VIDOR. I knew Freeman had an office because I'd been to it once, a fly-specked, dusty two-room suite in a crumbling building on Broadway straight out of Raymond Chandler, but he preferred to do business at bars. His favorite, a cop bar called the Code Seven, had gone out of business, but he'd found a replacement, an equally dark and gin-soaked dive on First Street called the Rolling Rock Cafe. He was already there when I arrived, at a corner table, peering over half-glasses at the stock market listings in the *Wall Street Journal*.

I'd known Freeman for seven years and he hadn't changed at all. He was a black man—he didn't go in for African-American—in late middle age, fast talking, reed-thin and very smart. He'd been a cop with the LAPD in the dark ages of Darryl Gates and his equally benighted predecessors, when racism had not only run rampant but had had the status of unofficial department policy. No unassuming Tom Bradley, Freeman had made waves and quickly found himself unpromotable, so he'd quit and gone into business for himself. He was very good at his work. He told me once the secret of his success as a private investigator was the same thing that worked against him as a cop, the assumption by white people that they were smarter than he was. It made them careless around him, which, as many of them subsequently discovered, was a real mistake.

We were friendly but not friends, because Freeman didn't have friends. That I was gay had never seemed to register with him one way or another. He was an equal-opportunity misanthrope.

"When did you start wearing glasses?" I asked, pulling out a chair across from him.

"When I got old," he said, folding the paper.

"You play the market?"

"It's my retirement," he replied. "You oughta start thinking about that."

"What would I retire to? My rose garden?"

"So, you're all tangled up with this dead judge," he said. "I hear the cops have got the boyfriend down for it. You working on a slow plea or do you have something up your sleeve?"

"He didn't do it," I said.

Freeman flashed his yellow teeth and signaled the waitress. "Double bourbon for me," he told her. "My friend will have a Roy Rogers."

"Coffee would be fine," I said.

When he was settled with his drink, he lit a Kool and said, "So?"

I told him the whole story.

"Go over that last part again," he said, when I was done. "The part that proves the boyfriend didn't do it."

"Not proof," I reminded him. "Reasonable doubt."

"Yeah, that part."

"Okay. Chris leaves the courthouse and goes out to meet someone for dinner, Mr. X. Chris has a lot to drink, maybe X does, too, and they return to the courthouse together. They quarrel. Chris turns his back on X, and X picks up the obelisk and knocks Chris down. He hits him a few more times, then, when he realizes he's killed him, he panics and runs. Some time later, Zack arrives, sees Chris on the ground. He picks up the obelisk and turns him over and sees that he's dead. Then Zack panics and leaves. X, meanwhile, has had time to calm down and realizes that his prints are on the obelisk. Maybe he's left other evidence, too, from which he could be identified, so he makes himself go back. Zack said he nearly collided with someone entering the court-house garage in a big, four-wheel-drive vehicle. Thinking about it last night, I realized the driver could've recognized Zack. Anyway, X removes the obelisk. Since he knows Zack was there, he decides to frame him for the murder and plant the obelisk at his apartment. Now, there's a period of a couple of days when Zack's apartment building is empty. X could've gotten into his apartment and left the obelisk without being detected. Then," I concluded, "he calls McBeth as the anonymous tipster and tells her about the obelisk and the bloody clothes. She gets the warrant, finds the stuff and arrests Zack."

"Wow," he said, rattling the ice in his drink. "You got everything but dancing bears." He took a sip and set the glass down. "Now, let me ask you a few questions."

I sat back and waited for him to tear my story apart. It's what I counted on him for.

"You don't know he went out to eat or where or if he was with someone or by himself."

"That's your job."

"I'll come back to that," he said. "You don't know if he came back to the court with someone or alone."

"A guard or someone else working late at the court might have seen him."

"Didn't the cops ask about that?"

"I don't have all their follow-up reports yet," I said. "I don't know who they may have talked to about Chris's movements."

"Your Mr. X, you think that's his kid, right? Jocy?"

"So far," I said.

"Because he's mad at his daddy for going gay? So he kills him?"

"He knew about the obelisk," I reminded him.

"According to you, you asked him the question, but he didn't answer you."

"I asked him if he knew his father had been killed with the award and he didn't deny it."

"Maybe that's because he didn't know what the hell you were talking about," Freeman said, lighting another cigarette.

"I was there. I saw his reaction. He knew."

"What about an alibi?"

I said, "As far as I know, the cops didn't question him, so he hasn't had to provide one."

"That doesn't mean he don't have one."

"Well, we'll have to find out, won't we? What about the car Zack saw? Joey drives a black Jeep Cherokee."

"Like it's the only one in the county of L.A."

"Chris's property was returned to the family," I said, having learned that fact earlier in the day. "That includes his key chain with the keys to Zack's apartment."

"How do you know Joey knew where he lived?"

"He called him once," I reminded him. "He must've got the number from Chris's address book. Maybe the address, too."

"How did he know your guy wasn't going to be in his apartment?"

"The building across the street from Zack's complex was on the front page of the *Times*," I said. "He could've have read the story or heard it on TV, recognized the address and figured out that all the adjacent buildings had been evacuated. Or maybe he didn't know, but took a chance and drove out there."

"How smart is this kid?" he asked, signaling for another round.

"I'm not saying this was all planned out," I replied. "It was a crime of passion. He killed his father in a rage, then started looking for a way out. Opportunities to frame Zack presented themselves and he took them. He had some lucky breaks, including the fact that the cops never suspected him. He wasn't even interviewed. Bay didn't mention that Chris had left her until the cops had already started to focus on Zack, and when she told him, she made a point of mentioning the will. That's all McBeth needed. That, plus the anonymous tip. The cops never looked twice at Joey, and now that Zack's been charged, their investigation's closed."

The waitress brought his drink. He sipped at it for a minute. "Why don't you think the boyfriend did it? Because he told you?"

"I've defended a lot of murderers," I said, "and you know what they had in common, Freeman? They were all a little dead themselves. Zack's just the opposite. The things he's been through should've killed him, but he kept himself alive."

"Is that what you're going to tell the jury?"

"No," I said. "I'm going to tell the jury he didn't have a motive."

"The will?"

I'd thought about that. "Chris changed his will within a month of the murder. How much sense does it make to murder someone who put you in his will before the ink's dry? Especially in such a sloppy way? You'd have to be pretty greedy and they can't prove that on Zack."

"What do you want me to do?"

"Find out about Chris's movements the night he was killed, especially where and with whom he had dinner."

"There's dozens of restaurants around the courthouse," he said.

"Whenever we had lunch we always went to a place called the Epicenter on Second and Hill. Start there. His clerk might know if he had any other favorites."

"Okay," he said, scratching a note on a cocktail napkin.

"Joey Chandler," I said. "He goes to USC. Talk to him there, not at his house."

"What about the wife?"

I shook my head. "Leave her out of this for now. She's an old friend."

A half-smile twisted his mouth. "Not after this."

I let it pass. "Joey probably won't be particularly cooperative, so you'll have to ask around him, friends, classmates."

"What else?"

"I want to retrace Zack's movements through the courthouse at night," I said. "To corroborate his story. I can't do it alone and then call myself to the witness stand, so let's meet there Friday night. That's the same day of the week Chris was killed."

"Okay, down in the garage off Olive?"

"Yeah, say about ten."

"You want me to check out Bowen's apartment building and talk to the tenants?"

"I'm going out there as soon as we finish here," I said. "There is one other thing, though. How are your lines to black officers on LAPD?"

"So-so," he said. "Most of the ones I came up with are collecting their pensions."

"I'd like you to find out what you can about McBeth."

"Like what?"

"I don't think she plays by the book," I said.

"If she did," he replied, "she'd be the first." He called for the check and handed it to me. "The meter's running," he said.

Karen Holman had agreed to meet at the apartment complex during her lunch break. I got to the building a few minutes before our appointment, slipped beneath the caution tape and went out to the courtyard, carrying the camera I kept in my trunk. The complex was designed to cram as many people as possible on a narrow, rectangular lot. There were twenty-two apartments in all, twelve on each floor. They were arranged four on each of the long sides of the rectangle and two on the short ones. The floors were connected by open stairwells at either end of the courtyard.

The exterior, stucco walls were white. The doors to the apartments were blue and numbered, 101 to 110 on the first floor and 201 to 210 on the second. A few feet from the doors were small sliding glass windows. I looked into one and saw a kitchen. Above each door was a light. Other than these, there were no sources of exterior light except in the stairwells.

I went up to the second floor, coming out of the stairwell in front of apartment 201, at the east end of the floor. Zack lived in 206, straight down the breezeway at the opposite end. McBeth's anonymous tipster said Zack had passed in front of his kitchen window. That meant his apartment was on the north side of the second floor, 202 to 205, rather than across the courtyard on the south side, 208 to 211. While it was possible that Zack could've been seen by someone standing at the window of one of those apartments, his view would've been obstructed by the waist-high retaining wall that ran the length of the second-floor breezeway. Additionally, he would have been looking across the courtyard, a distance of a couple of hundred feet. The tipster's observations were too detailed to have been made by someone watching from that distance and with the wall between him and Zack. No, it had to be someone in one of the north-side apartments. I walked to the first window and stood there. I couldn't see in, because the blinds were drawn, but I noticed immediately that the window was level with my chest. Zack was shorter than me by three or four inches. How could someone standing on the other side of the window have seen what was in his hands?

And the tipster hadn't been standing. According to McBeth's affidavit, he'd been sitting at the kitchen table.

19

I HEARD THE CLATTER OF FOOTSTEPS BEHIND ME.

"Mr. Rios?" Karen Holman said. She wore a white silk blouse, a gray skirt and low heels, the anonymous costume of a low-ranking office worker. I remembered she'd told me on the phone she worked for an escrow company.

"Hi," I said. "Thanks for meeting me on such short notice."

"No problem," she said. "Real estate's dead. Anyway, I was going to call you, because the owners want everyone moved out by the end of the week and you said you'd take care of Zack's stuff."

"Are they going to tear down the building?"

She frowned. "That's what they say. I think it's a scam to get around rent control."

"You mean they'd get rid of the present tenants, then jack up the rents and find new ones? What about the damage to the foundation?"

"I know a contractor," she said. "I asked him to come out and take a look around. He couldn't find any structural damage, just some cracks is all. Nothing serious."

"Have you filed a complaint with the city?"

"I wouldn't know where to begin," she said.

"Building and safety?" I suggested. "The rent control board."

"That takes time," she said, "and they want us out now. We all got letters yesterday."

"The other tenants aren't even here," I said.

"I know, I know," she said, her cheeks flushing with anger. "It's just plain shitty, but that's what the owners are like. I don't what I'm going to do. They give me a four-hundred-dollar break on my rent to manage the place. I don't know where I'm going to find a two-bedroom that cheap around here. I don't want to move and have to take Teddy out of his school."

"I know a Legal Aid lawyer who does tenant-landlord work. If you want, I could put you in touch with him. It won't cost you anything and it sounds to me like you've got a case."

"Can't they fire me if I give them trouble?"

"Matt wouldn't let them get away with something like that," I said.

"Matt?"

"Matt Chin, my Legal Aid lawyer friend. Look, I'll call him as soon as we're finished."

"That would be great," she said, visibly relieved. "So, how can I help you?"

"Someone told the police they saw Zack coming back to his apartment the night Chris Chandler was murdered," I said. "I want to know who it was."

"Don't the police know?"

"It was an anonymous call," I replied. "The caller said he was afraid Zack might take revenge."

She clucked, "That's ridiculous. Zack's like the last person in the world who would hurt anyone. And we've had our share of assholes around here but people don't spy on each other."

"I'm interested in the four apartments along this hallway," I said. "Who lives in them?"

We were standing in front of 202. "No one lives here," she said. "Thank God. The last tenant was one of the assholes I was talking about and he left at the end of September."

"Two-oh-three?" I asked, walking toward it.

"The girls," she said. "Joan Woods and Darlene Sawyer." She smiled indulgently. "Actresses."

"Actress-waitress-whatevers?"

"You got it," she said.

"Do you know where they are now?"

"Joan's gone," she said. "She split the day after the quake back to Michigan where she's from. She said she'd had enough, what with riots, earthquakes and fires. Darlene's staying with some friends in Hollywood. I've got all the information downstairs."

"Okay," I said. "What about two-oh-four."

"The Wards," she said. "Don and Donna. Honest to God. An older black couple. Really nice. They're staying with one of their kids. I've got a number for them, too."

"Is Mr. Ward the kind of guy who makes anonymous calls to the cops about his neighbors?" I asked her.

She shook her head. "Don's no chickenshit. If he's got something to say, he says it. Anyway, they were both friendly with Zack. They wouldn't be afraid of him."

"Two-oh-five?"

"Ben Harper," she said. "Drives a truck for UPS and lives at the gym when he's not. He gets a little loud with his music when he's had a few beers, but he's all right." The color crept back into her cheeks. "I dated him a couple of times."

"You have a falling-out?"

Her laughter was unexpectedly raucous. "No, nothing like that. I just couldn't compete."

"Another woman?"

"His mirror," she said.

"I know the type," I said. "Was he friendly with Zack?"

"No, I wouldn't say that," she replied. "Zack's the one who complained about Ben's music and I think Zack made Ben nervous, being gay and all."

"Nervous enough to rat him out?"

"If he did, he wouldn't do it behind Zack's back," she said. "Ben's a big boy. He's not afraid of anyone."

"You know where he is?"

"Yeah, just down the street at the Double Palms motel." She smiled crookedly. "Room one-oh-nine."

•   •   •

We went down to her apartment, where she gave me phone numbers for Darlene Sawyer, the Wards and Ben Harper. I called Matt Chin who, after talking it over with her, agreed to get in touch with the owners about the situation at the building. She thanked me, and again said she'd do anything she could to help Zack.

"I may need you to testify at a hearing in a couple of weeks," I said.

"Okay," she said. "Just give me something to take to my boss so I can get the time off."

"I'll get you a subpoena," I said.

I went and sat in my car for a moment. McBeth's tipster was male. That let out the two women in 203, unless one of them had had a male guest that night, so it was either Don Ward on 204 or Ben Harper in 205. I got on the phone and starting calling the numbers Karen Holman had given me.

I'd expected to reach answering machines but, surprisingly, both Don Ward and Darlene Sawyer were at home and agreed to see me. I left a message for Ben Harper at his motel.

Mr. Ward had warned me he had a cold and when I got to his daughter's house in Culver City, where he and his wife were staying, he greeted me in a bathrobe with swollen eyes and the sniffles. He was not a tall man, but he was powerfully built and, even with hair more gray than black, didn't look old enough to have an adult daughter. He brought me into a comfortably furnished living room and listened intently as I explained in greater detail why I'd come to see him.

"So you want to know if I called the police on Zack?" he said, when I'd finished.

"Did you?"

He pulled a tissue from the box of Kleenex on the table between us and blew his nose. "Excuse me," he said, "there's some shit in the air that's making people sick. They said on the news the quake shook it out of the ground." He wadded the tissue and tossed it into a paper bag beside his chair. "Now, Mr. Rios, you say this fella told the police he saw Zack at one o'clock in the morning the night of the quake. Well, at one o'clock in the morning I was sound asleep in bed with my wife."

"So you didn't make that call?"

"Let me explain something," he said. "Zack's a good boy. I know he's queer, but he never bothered me with any of that stuff and he's always been polite and respectful, so even if I did see something like that, I'd forget about it."

"But you didn't," I pressed.

"No, I was dead to the world until my wife woke me up screaming for Jesus."

"Would you testify to that?"

He regarded me suspiciously. "You mean in court?"

I nodded.

"Well, I can't say that I would," he replied. "I mean, I didn't see nothing, so it's none of my business."

"I need to prove that the person who called the police wasn't a tenant," I said.

"You said they found things at Zack's apartment," he said. "What does it matter who told the police? I mean, if the boy killed the man, he should pay the consequences."

"Mr. Ward, does Zack seem like a killer to you?"

He reached for another Kleenex to cover a loud sneeze. "Bless you," I said.

"Thanks," he said. "Well, Zack don't seem much like a killer to me, that's true. But, hell, gays kill each other. Just look at that guy they put in the gas chamber up in Illinois. Gacy."

Great, I thought, now we're all potential serial killers, as if every straight guy was a potential Ted Bundy.

"I'm talking about Zack Bowen," I said, playing to his prejudices. "This is a kid who collects ceramic turtles and sews his own curtains."

"Yeah, he is kind of a sissy. But if he didn't kill the guy, how did that stuff get in his apartment?"

"What I think is that the cops were eager to make an arrest and they went after the obvious target without doing much of an investigation."

"Yeah," he mused. "That's what they said about O.J."

"All I'm asking you to do is testify that you didn't make that call. I'll keep the inconvenience to a minimum and you'll help keep an innocent man from going to jail."

"Would I be on TV?"

Simpson, again, I thought, the trial that had forever corrupted the criminal justice system.

"I don't know," I answered, truthfully.

"Leave me your card," he said, "and I'll talk to my wife about it and we'll get back to you." He sneezed. "And be careful of the air."

From Culver City I drove back to West Hollywood, where Darlene Sawyer was staying with friends on a street not far from where Josh lived. I'd expected Sawyer to be one of the legion of pretty, aerobicized twenty-something would-be actors who roamed L.A. with glossy head shots and perfect orthodontics. Instead, I found a thin woman in her mid-thirties with a frank, intelligent face and a whiskey voice. She ushered me into a plant-filled living room, offered me coffee, lit up a Virginia Slim and said, "So, who framed Zack Bowen?"

"I beg your pardon?"

She exhaled smoke and smiled, showing small, yellowed teeth. "You're his attorney," she said. "You must know he didn't kill Chris."

"You, either?"

"Honey," she said, "Zack loved that man, and he was good for him. It doesn't make any sense that he'd hurt him."

"Nonetheless," I said, "someone in your building said he saw Zack on the night of the murder wearing a bloody shirt and carrying the object that was used to kill Chris."

"Well, it wasn't me," she said.

"No, the police said the anonymous caller was male. That lets you and your ex-roommate," I glanced at my notes, "Joan Woods, off the hook. Unless either of you had a male visitor that night."

She laughed. "Flatterer," she said.

"So the answer's no."

"Joan and I ate dinner, watched a tape of *The Awful Truth* and were in bed by ten." She smiled crookedly. "Our respective beds, I mean. No funny business there."

"And the next day Ms. Woods returned to Michigan?"

"It was a couple of days later," she said. "The earthquake worked her last nerve. I can't say I blame her. L.A.'s a scary place even when the earth isn't trying to swallow you whole."

I liked her. She had the air of someone who'd been battered around the edges and didn't give a damn about appearances. A truth-teller, so I asked her what she thought of Zack and Chris as a couple.

She gave it some thought. "Zack's a little hunk, of course, but not the world's most sophisticated guy, so when Chris first started coming around I assumed he was taking out his midlife crisis on Zack and I was all set not to like him." She fanned wisps of smoke from her face. "But it wasn't like that. Chris cared for him. I mean, I don't know that it would've been a long-term thing, they were very different men, but the feeling between them was real."

"How could you tell?"

"Darling, feelings are my metier," she said. "I absorb them and save them up so I can call on them when I'm performing. I paid attention to Chris and Zack and it was a very sweet thing to see. Chris was a bit on the stodgy side, like you, love, if you don't mind my saying so, but around Zack he was like a schoolkid with his first big crush and Zack was so proud and so happy." Worry flickered across her face. "Where is Zack? How is he?"

"He's at the men's jail downtown," I said. "He's holding up as well as can be expected."

"Will they let me visit him?"

"Yes, and I'm sure he'd appreciate it," I said. "Do you think Don Ward might have been the anonymous tipster who called the cops?"

"No, not Don. He's kind of homophobic, but it's in that passive way of pretending not to notice, you know what I mean? As if by ignoring gay people, they don't exist. He wouldn't want to get mixed up in anything that happened between Chris and Zack. And anyway his wife, Donna, was very sweet on Zack, so she wouldn't let Don do anything to hurt him."

"What do you mean she was sweet on Zack?"

She laughed. "You dirty man. Think maternal, not erotic. Donna's a motherly woman and Zack was clearly a boy in need of mothering. Even I was known to wipe the smudge off his cheek from time to time."

"What about Ben Harper?"

"A himbo," she said. "You know, a male bimbo? His tits are bigger than mine, but when it comes to IQ we're talking double digits at best. Zack made him nervous because he's as buff as Ben, only he's a queer, and Ben worried about guilt by association. But did he call the cops? Only if someone else dialed for him."

"I may need you to testify."

"Great, where do I sign up? I've always wanted to be a witness. Maybe the exposure will give me a career break." She laughed again. "I mean, it worked for Kato Kaelin, didn't it?"

It took me another day to catch up with Ben Harper. He was staying at a place called the Double Palms Motel, not far from the apartment complex. Ben Harper was the first man I'd ever met for whom Fabio was a role model. He had the same height, girth, long blond hair and musculature of the man who'd risen from the cover of romance novels to fame and fortune and, just like Fabio, Harper liked to show it off. Tight black jeans, muscle shirt and skin that was unnaturally tan even by L.A. standards. As he thrust a big, calloused hand at me, I couldn't help but think Sam Bligh could give this guy a career in the movies.

"You Mr. Rios?" he said, in a surprisingly pleasant tenor.

"Yes," I said, submitting to a bone-crushing handshake. "Thanks for talking to me, Mr. Harper."

"Ben," he said. "Come on in. The place is kind of a mess."

It was a standard motel room, vaguely southwestern in decor, with a queen-sized bed, bureau, TV and a couple of chairs. There were clothes everywhere, a jock strap hung from the doorknob, the remnants of fast-food meals overflowed the wastebasket and a dozen empty Dos Equis bottles lined the window sill.

"Have a seat," he said.

I took the only chair in the room that wasn't piled with clothes while he sat at the edge of the bed. His long, narrow face would've been handsome had there been a glimmer of anything in it, but he was as blank as an animal.

"I won't take up too much of your time," I said. "I told you on the phone I'm Zack Bowen's lawyer. You know he's in jail on a murder charge."

He nodded his head with every word. "Huh-uh. Yeah, I heard from Karen. Too bad."

"The police got an anonymous call from someone claiming to be one of Zack's neighbors, saying that he saw Zack the night of the murder carrying what the police think was the murder weapon. I wondered if you made that call?"

"Nope," he said, without a moment's hesitation.

"It was the night of the earthquake," I said. "Around one in the morning. Were you at home?"

He shrugged his mountainous shoulders. "Guess so. Probably, but I didn't see a thing."

"That's odd," I said, "because none of the other tenants saw anything either. So it was either you or no one."

It took him a minute to work this out. "So what are you saying, that I'm lying?"

"You didn't like Zack much, did you?"

He fidgeted. "Didn't think about it one way or the other."

"I'm not accusing you of anything, Ben," I said. "If you didn't like him, you didn't like him. It's your right."

This seemed to register. "Damn right it's my right," he said. "I don't like fags, okay? No law against that."

"No, but you're not afraid of them, either, are you?"

"Say what?" he said incredulously.

"The police say the reason the caller wouldn't identify himself was because he was afraid Zack might get back at him."

"Shit," he said, smiling hugely. "I could break that little fag over my knee."

"So if you had seen anything and called the cops, you would've identified yourself to them, right?"

"Didn't call 'em," he said, reverting to monosyllables. "Didn't see a damn thing. Was probably asleep." He grinned. "Or beatin' off."

There was no innuendo in this statement; it was just his way of making small talk.

"Would you swear to it?"

He raised his right hand in a Boy Scout salute. "I swear."

"In court?"

He dropped his hand and said, "Hey, man, I work for a living. I can't be taking time off to go down to court."

"It won't take long," I said. "I'm sure your employer would understand if I subpoenaed you."

"If you what?"

"A subpoena is an order from the court requiring a person to come and testify."

"And what if I just tear it up," he said.

"Ben," I said, "we're talking about a murder trial. You're very important, not just to me, but to the D.A. Without you, we might not be able to get to the truth. You're kind of a star witness."

He very nearly preened. "Do I get paid?"

"Yeah, there are witness fees. Not much, but then your employer might be persuaded to give you the time off with pay. For doing your duty as a citizen."

He thought it over. "Yeah, sure, what the hell. When do you want me?"

"A couple of weeks," I said. "I'll get that subpoena to you. If there's any problem with your bosses, any problem at all, you let me know."

"Is he gonna get off?" he asked.

"Who? Zack? I don't know."

"Because if he did it, he should get the chair."

I got up to go. "That's for the jury to decide. Thanks for your time."

As I replayed the interview in my head on the way home I was pretty sure that Harper was lying, but I didn't know about what. Since he was no friend of Zack's, and wasn't afraid of him, he had no reason to lie to me about having made the call to the cops, unless he hadn't figured out that by doing so he would be helping Zack. If that was the case, I could only hope he wouldn't add it up before the hearing. Still, it was hard to imagine why he would've called anonymously. The obvious possibility was that it was the cops he was afraid of, rather than Zack. I made a mental note to see if he had a prior criminal record.

If he was telling the truth, then that meant that none of Zack's neighbors was the anonymous tipster. That was clear even from a comparison of the physical layout of the complex with the tipster's account of how he had seen Zack. There was no way someone sitting at a table in the kitchen could have seen Zack passing by the window and carrying the obelisk in his hand unless he was holding his hand out in front of him. Yet the tipster did have a general idea of what the building looked like, so he had obviously been there.

To plant evidence, I thought.

20

A COUPLE OF NIGHTS LATER, I FOUND MYSELF STANDING AT THE entrance to the underground garage at the municipal courthouse, waiting for Freeman Vidor. A long driveway descended from the street into the garage, and above the entrance were signs warning that parking was restricted to permit parkers and all others would be towed. To my right was a shuttered guardhouse. As usual at that hour, downtown was nearly deserted. At half past ten, Freeman emerged from the garage, smoking a cigarette.

"Ready to break in?" he asked.

"What were you doing in the garage?"

"Checking out security," he said. He crushed the cigarette on the ground.

"Is it tight?"

He smirked and said, "You'll see. Come on."

The garage was a vast, echoing subterreanean space that not only provided parking for court employees but also county workers in nearby buildings. Except for Freeman's black Jaguar, which he'd parked in a handicap space, the few cars visible all had parking permits on their back fenders.

"The lot goes beneath Olive," he was saying, indicating the dark reaches of the place. "The way we came down is the only entrance and there's just one exit, to Temple. You notice the guardhouse at the top of the driveway?"

"Yes," I said. "It looks abandoned."

"There's a guard up there during the day," he said. "You have to have a permit to park down here and he'll stop you if you don't and turn you around. If he misses you, there's a patrol that goes around, and if they find a car without a permit they tow it."

I gestured to his car and said, "Evidently they don't patrol at night."

"They did," he said, "but the county runs the courthouse and the county's bankrupt. They cut out the night patrols a year ago."

"Is that why there's no one at the guardhouse, either?"

"Yeah," he said. "I guess the county can't afford the overtime." He headed toward a pair of double metal doors recessed into a concrete wall. "The doors into the courthouse. Try 'em."

I grabbed a metal handle and pulled. The door opened. "Just like that? Where's the security?"

"Here," Freeman said, pointing to a device in the wall which had the dimensions and appearance of a bathroom mirror with a metal shelf at the bottom of it. Smoked glass covered both the mirrorlike rectangle on the wall and the shelf. "There's a camera behind the glass that's supposed to let the marshals upstairs see who's down here. Then you put your ID card here," he continued, indicating the shelf. "A scanner reads your card and they match you up with your picture and buzz you in through the doors. Problem is, the camera's broken."

"In the earthquake?"

"I doubt it," he said. "If they were using it before the quake, they'd have fixed it up by now. And look how the door sticks."

I let the door drop. It wedged slightly against the other door. "So?"

"Defeats the purpose of the buzzer," he said. "I'd say this system broke down before the quake and they didn't have the money to fix it."

"So basically," I said, "anyone who knows about this entrance can walk into the courthouse?"

"That's about the size of it," he said. "Of course, the only people who are going to know about it are the people who are supposed to be down here in the first place. Employees. The public entrance is upstairs on the street. I guess that's why they figured they could let this go." He opened the door. "After you?"

The doors opened to a wide corridor that led to another door marked

"Stairs." It was not locked. Two short flights of stairs and another door and we found ourselves on the ground floor of the courthouse.

"Zack said Chris told him if he was stopped by a security guard to tell him that he was going to see Chris," I said. "That implies there are guards. Are there?"

"Yeah," Freeman said, as he led us around the corner to a bank of elevators. "Down there."

The courthouse occupied nearly an entire block and its scale was, accordingly, gargantuan. At the end of the wide corridor from where we were standing, about half the distance of a football field, a blue-coated security guard was sitting at a desk at the front entrance of the courthouse, his back to us. We could've exploded grenades without attracting his attention. Freeman pressed the elevator button and the door slid open. We boarded the elevator. The whole thing took less than thirty seconds. "Which floor?"

"Five," I said.

The fifth floor was empty. The polished linoleum was still damp from mopping and the big brass lights blazed overhead. Alternating double and single doors ran the length of the walls, which were faced with marble. The double doors were the public entrances into the courtrooms and each was marked in gold lettering with the number of the courtroom and the judge who presided therein. The single doors were not marked. They were the private entrances into the judges' chambers, which were located behind the courtrooms. The place was as still as a mausoleum as we made our way down the hall past the doors to Chris's courtroom, which still bore his name, to the unmarked door that led to his chambers. I grabbed the doorknob confidently but this time the door did not yield.

"What do you know," I said, jiggling the knob. "A lock that actually works."

"American Express," Freeman said, slipping a credit card between the frame and the door. "Don't leave home without it."

I heard a click and then he pulled the door open.

"Nice work," I said. "Of course, Chris was expecting Zack, so this door would've been unlocked."

We found ourselves in a dark hallway. I ran my hand along the wall until I found the light switch and flipped it on. We walked to the end of the hall where it intersected another, shorter, corridor which led, in either direction, to a door. Chris's name was visible on the right-hand door. Freeman did his credit card trick on it and got us inside. I clicked the light on. The surfaces of the room were covered with the fine black powder used by the cops to lift prints. There was a dark stain on the carpet beside the desk. All of Chris's personal items had been stripped from the room. I glanced into the small bathroom; even his hand towels had been removed. For the first time, I felt spooked.

"Ten minutes," Freeman said, glancing at his watch.

"Huh?"

"It took us ten minutes to get up here from the garage."

"And no one saw us," I said. "How is that possible?"

Freeman perched at the edge of the desk. "A couple of days ago I called the court administrator and said I ran a private security company and I was interested in bidding for this job, seeing that a judge had been knocked off," he said. "He's the one who told me about all the cutbacks because of the budget. When I asked him what precautions he was taking since the murder, he said he issued a memo warning people against working in the building after six, when it closes to the public. Otherwise, they've got five guards patroling all ten floors from six to midnight."

"And after midnight?"

He smiled. "They lock up and go home."

"How often are the patrols?"

"Supposedly on the hour," he said.

"Amazing," I said. "This place is wide open."

At that moment, I heard footsteps in the hall.

Freeman glanced at his watch. "It's a quarter to. They're early."

"Ten floors and they pick on us," I said, hitting the light switch in the room. "Quick, into the bathroom."

I left the bathroom door open a crack and stood back so that, while I was in the darkness, a sliver of the outer room was visible to me. Someone entered the chambers and turned the light on. I glimpsed a blue-clad back as the guard passed in front of the bathroom door. I was aware that both Freeman and I had stopped breathing. I ran through the story I would tell if we were discovered, but then he passed in front of the door again, turned the light out and left. I waited another moment, until I could no longer hear his footsteps, before I let us out of the bathroom.

"They don't exactly break their necks around here to secure the place," Freeman observed.

"No," I agreed, "but why would they? A courthouse must run pretty low on the list of potential crime targets."

"Except that this happened," he said, indicating the rusty stain on the carpet.

"True," I said, "but it's random crime you guard against, and Chris's murder wasn't random."

"We through here?" Freeman asked. "This case gives me the willies."

I was standing at the door, facing Chris's desk, trying to imagine what Zack had seen when he entered the room that night. A body on the ground, blood, the pointed end of the obelisk embedded in the back of Chris's skull. Seeing the room, remembering his description, something flickered through my head, not quite a thought, not quite a memory, and it came out of my mouth as, "Someone saw him."

Freeman said, "What?"

"Nothing," I said, because I didn't understand myself what I meant. "You're right. It's creepy. Let's get out of here."

We got out of the building undetected. Back in the garage, I walked Freeman to his car.

"Want a lift?" he asked.

"No, I'm just out on the street. Have you had any luck finding out whether Chris had dinner with someone the night he was killed?"

He shook his head. "I got his clerk to give me the names of his five favorite restaurants, but I haven't finished checking them out."

"What about the Epicenter?" I asked.

"It's on my list," he said.

"Have you talked to Joey Chandler?"

"Tried to," he grunted. "I did like you suggested and went out to USC and caught him between classes. He wanted to know if I was the police and when I told him I wasn't, he said he didn't have to talk to me. Period."

"So we still don't know if he has an alibi or not?"

"Nope," he agreed.

"And McBeth? What did you find out about her?"

"She's a detective two," he said, "and she got there in record time."

"What's her reputation?"

"She's a black woman on the fast track," he said. "What do you think? Her brothers in blue figure she's an affirmative action baby and they don't like that. Plus, she's cozy with the chief and you know how most of the rank-and-file feel about him."

I nodded. The current chief was a black man brought in from the outside after Darryl Gates had been forced to resign following the Rodney King fiasco. He was deeply unpopular, particularly with white and Latino officers who accused him of favoring African-Americans. Relationships between those groups had deteriorated to the point that the black police officer association had brought a civil-rights action against the police union in federal court.

"What about her work? Is she a corner-cutter?"

"She's ambitious," he said. "Ambition affects different people in different ways. Some get extra-careful, some fudge a little."

"And McBeth?"

"No major beefs there, but you know that there's people laying in wait."

"Yeah," I said, "and this is a big case for her."

Freeman grinned. "I'd hate to be the guy that brought a sister down."

"I could give this piece of the investigation to someone else."

"Screw it," he said, lighting a Kool. "I never claimed to be politically correct."

"No," I said, "that's my job."

"Yeah," he agreed. "You're kind of a poster child for the politically correct, aren't you?"

"Keep in touch," I said. He got into his car and gunned his way out of the lot.

That night, I had a dream. In the dream, I found myself in the garage. It was dark and empty and as I stood there it seemed to close in on me until, in a panic, I started searching for a way out. In the distance, I saw a door. The door was cracked open enough to see there was light on the other side. I walked toward it, feeling the darkness tighten around me. I reached the door, but when I raised my hand to pull it open, something stopped me, a noise coming from the other side. It was a squishy sound, like the sound of something trying to pull itself out of the mud. I knelt down and peered through the crack and saw Chris Chandler sprawled on the floor while a man knelt over him and slammed a marble obelisk into the back of his head, making the soft, muddy noise I had heard. The man's back was to me and I could see nothing of his face. Jets of blood sprayed the walls. I recoiled and bumped into someone who had come in the darkness behind me. I turned and looked. It was Joey Chandler.

The next morning, as I was still puzzling over the meaning of the dream, the phone rang. I picked it up and before I could speak, a woman said, "Please hold for Joseph Kimball."

A moment later, Chris's father-in-law, Ray's father and one of the most powerful lawyers in the city was saying, "Henry? Joe Kimball here. I think we need to talk."

He made it sound as if we chatted regularly when, in fact, I had probably spoken to him a dozen times in twenty years.

"What can I do for you, Mr. Kimball?"

"Your investigator was out at USC talking to my grandson."

"That's right," I said. "I'm representing the man accused of murdering Chris."

"So I'm given to understand," he said, with faint but unmistakable distaste. "I don't know what possible light Joey can shed on your defense of this man."

"If he'd talked to my investigator it would've become apparent."

There was a pause. "You know, my daughter asked me to call you because she's too angry to speak to you herself."

"I'm sorry to hear that," I said. "I don't mean to hurt her any further, but I don't believe my client killed Chris and I'm obliged to pursue every possible avenue of defense."

"And which avenue takes you to my grandson?"

"This is not something I want to discuss on the phone," I replied.

Another pause. "I see. Could you come to my office tomorrow morning? Say, eleven."

"That will be fine," I said.

"Good," he said. "See you then."

I put the phone down. Joe Kimball was out of the reach of most mortals. He didn't so much practice law as trade favors, and they were the kind of favors for which rules were bent and formalities overlooked. He wouldn't have called unless he was ready to deal, and he made the kind of offers that one could not refuse.

The elevator deposited me at Kimball's law offices on the twenty-third floor of the Wells Fargo Building. The windows of the foyer looked out upon the palm-tree-dotted, sun-baked, polyglot sprawl that was Los Angeles. The room's furnishings evoked a different world, with its dark woods, deep carpeting and eighteenth-century ancestor portraits, as if Kimball's firm consisted of solicitous pin-striped-suited gentlemen who spent their days revising codicils for elderly widows. In fact, however, Kimball & Casey employed four hundred lawyers in a half-dozen offices across the state working tirelessly on behalf of banks, big businesses and the handful of exceedingly rich individuals who could afford Kimball's hourly rates.

This was the world Chris had inhabited before he became a judge. Joe Kimball had taken to him like a son and his rise through the firm had been meteoric and, he liked to point out, merited. Still, as Kimball's son-in-law, he had been something of an heir apparent and he had been treated as such by the other partners and the young associates who fought for his attention. He'd enjoyed that, just as he'd enjoyed the trappings of his success. More than the pleasure he got from them, they were proof that he'd made the right decision when he'd married Bay. He was right that, had he been openly gay, he would never have achieved the same level of success in the clubby culture of the city's ruling class. I never saw that it was the worth of sacrifice. There's a line from A Man for All Seasons, near the end of the play, when the protagonist, Sir Thomas More, remarks to a man who has perjured himself and sealed More's doom in exchange for the governorship of Wales that it profited a man nothing to give his soul for the whole world, "but for Wales?" That summed up my feelings about Chris's membership in this particular club.

"Mr. Kimball will see you now," the receptionist murmured. "His office is at the end of the hall."

The first time I laid eyes on Joe Kimball, when I was still a law student, I'd christened him, privately, the silver man. His hair was silver, as were his gray eyes in a certain light, and he was wearing a beautifully cut silvery-gray suit. As he rose from behind his desk to greet me, he was still silvery and smooth, though I realized he must now be in his late sixties or early seventies. Since it was Saturday he wore khakis and a blue blazer over a pink polo shirt, but even casually dressed he had the air of a man accustomed to deference. I recognized in his appearance the jocular masculinity that prevails among the men of the old rich, for whom pink is an amusing color for men's shirts but homosexuality is gender treason.

His was a bastion of male privilege in which women functioned mainly as decoration. It was true that his firm had a small number of women partners, but they were window dressing. I knew this not from Chris but from Bay, who had all her life felt discounted by her father because she was female. She once told me that it seemed her entire purpose had been to marry and bring a son into the family.

Sometime in the last decade, I remembered, Kimball's wife had died and he'd remarried a woman twenty years his junior. There was the obligatory silver-framed photograph of her on the credenza behind his desk, along with others of Bay and Joey, but none of Chris. The new wife was pictured in jodhpurs on a chestnut horse, riding crop in hand. Her smile was slightly impatient and a little forced. His, as he offered me coffee, was one of practiced sincerity.

"Yes," I said. "Black, please."

"Good man," he replied, picked up the phone and requested two cups.

A moment later, a thirtyish ash-blonde in a yellow cashmere cable-knit sweater and cream-colored slacks brought in a tray with the coffee poured into fragile bone china. She set them down before us and asked, "Anything else?"

"No, that's all," he said, smiling at her with a sexual warmth. She basked in that smile. I wondered if the jodhpured wife knew.

I sipped his excellent coffee, thanked him for making time to see me, and added, "Also, I wanted to express my sympathy to you on Chris's death."

His expression curdled. "Yes, it was a shock," he said. "But you didn't come here for condolences."

"No," I said. "I came here to talk about Joey. You know I'm defending Zack Bowen, the man accused of killing Chris."

"Bowen," he said, "I went to school with someone by that name."

"I doubt it's the same family," I replied. "The preliminary hearing's set for next week. I've made a motion to suppress certain evidence and unless I prevail on it, I imagine he'll be held to answer and a trial date set."

"I do know something about criminal procedure," he said a bit impatiently.

"My client is innocent," I said, forging on. "He had no reason to kill Chris, but your grandson did."

He sat back in his chair, the leather yielding to his imposing frame. "That's ridiculous," he said.

"Mr. Kimball, I'm not the police and I'm not the prosecutor. It's not my job to bring Chris's killer to justice, whatever that may mean in this situation. My job is to get my client off and I'll do it any way I can, but I'd rather not implicate Joey in the process."

He stared at me with chilly displeasure. It was as if a cloud was passing over the sun. "Do you have evidence of this absurd claim against my grandson?"

"I do," I said.

"What is it?"

"You know I can't answer that," I said, "but the evidence does exist. I will say at this point it's not strong enough to convict, but that's not my problem. All I have to do is create a reasonable doubt that Zack Bowen killed Chris. The evidence of Joey's involvement is strong enough for that purpose."

Kimball regarded me with something like amusement and said, "So you think you can get your client acquitted by resorting to the character assassination of a twenty-year-old boy who's just lost his father? That won't get you very far."

"Joey was seen entering the courthouse garage on the night Chris was murdered," I said, bluffing.

"Seen by whom?" The words were no sooner out of his mouth than he realized his mistake and said, with suave certainty, "He couldn't have been seen by anyone, because he wasn't there."

"My witness will testify to it," I replied.

I could see him considering his possible responses, searching for the least incriminating one.

"Your witness is mistaken," he said, with the same smooth tone.

"Joey will have to get on the stand and say so," I replied. "And then it won't be my investigator questioning him, it'll be me."

He changed gears and said, "If you're so sure it was my grandson who killed Chandler, why haven't you gone to the police with your evidence?"

"I told you," I replied, "that's not my job."

"But it is your job to exonerate your client," he said, "and if you can do that by revealing the real culprit, why not go to the authorities?"

"Is that really what you want me to do?"

"What else did you have in mind?"

"With the proper groundwork, Joey could get off fairly lightly if he came forward on his own."

"What do you mean, with the proper groundwork?"

"Chris's murder was a crime of passion," I replied. "A good lawyer and a persuasive psychiatrist could get Joey off with manslaughter and he'd be out in three years. Maybe it needn't even go that far if the D.A. was willing to cut a deal."

He listened intently, but when I finished, he said, "Tell me about this suppression motion. What are you after there?"

Without going into specifics, I explained that I had pretty good evidence to impeach McBeth's claim in her affidavit that she'd been directed to Zack's apartment by an anonymous tip.

"And who's the judge that's going to hear this?" Kimball asked.

"Torres-Jones," I said.

"I don't think I know him," he said.

"Her," I replied.

"Her," he repeated. "And if you suppress this evidence, the case against your client falls apart."

"That's right," I said.

"Well, maybe you'll get lucky at your hearing," he said, dismissively. "You'll have to excuse me, now. I have another appointment."

I got up and said, "Thank you for your time."

"Good luck," he smiled.

I stood for a moment in the hall outside of his office, just long enough to hear him pick up his phone and say, "Hi, it's grandad. Is your mother home?"

I would've stood there longer, but the woman in the yellow sweater appeared in the corridor and I made my exit.

I didn't know exactly what to make of my conversation with Joe Kimball but one thing was clear, Joey didn't have an alibi for the night of Chris's murder. If he had, Kimball would have laid it out and shown me to the door. Instead, what I got from him was an ambivalent mixture of indignation and calculation, as if he couldn't decide whether he wanted to intimidate me or cut a deal. I could see his dilemma. Legally, there was nothing he could do to prevent me from implicating Joey in Chris's murder because Joey wasn't a party to the case. Therefore, if I had evidence against Joey, he couldn't prevent its admission or challenge its veracity in court. His only possible solution was to persuade me not to use the evidence. He hadn't succeeded in scaring me off, but I was pretty sure I'd be hearing from him or Bay again.

21

THE BAILIFF, A SKINNY, RED-HEADED BOY, ON HEARING THE BUZZER that indicated the judge was about to enter the court, said, "Please rise, Division Twenty-four of the Municipal Court of Los Angeles is now in session, Judge Torres-Jones presiding."

I nudged Zack and we got to our feet. Torres-Jones was taller than I thought she'd be, but otherwise as benign in the flesh as she was in her photograph and she wore her authority with an easy self-confidence.

"Good morning," she said. "Please be seated."

I glanced back to the rows of benches behind the railing where witnesses and spectators sat, to see if the last of my witnesses, Karen Holman, had appeared yet. Don Ward was whispering something to his wife, Donna, who nodded agreement. Ben Harper sat apart, his arms crossed, trying to look unimpressed. Darlene Sawyer smiled at me from the back of the room. There were maybe a dozen other people in the room, some of from the press, the others, prosecution witnesses for the prelim. No Karen Holman.

I was sitting at counsel table with Zack, who was wearing a coat and tie for the occasion. At the other end of the table, the D.A., an intense, curly-haired woman named Laura Lang, conferred with Yolanda Mc-Beth, both of them in dark suits. McBeth glanced over at me, then quickly looked away.

The judge was saying, "People versus Bowen. The defendant is present in court. Will the parties state their appearances for the record."

"Henry Rios for the defendant," I said.

"Laura Lang for the People."

"Thank you," the judge said. "We're here this morning for the pre-liminary hearing and also for a fifteen-thirty-eight-point-five motion. Shall we take the motion first?"

"That would be the defense's preference, Your Honor," I said.

She looked at Lang, "People?"

"That's fine," she said.

"All right, let's proceed. Mr. Rios, it's your motion. Proceed."

"Yes, Your Honor," I said, getting to my feet. "Unlike most suppres-sion hearings, there is a search warrant in this case. We are seeking to have the warrant quashed on the grounds that the supporting affidavit contains either deliberate falsehoods or was made with a reckless dis-regard for the truth. We want to suppress all evidence gathered as a result of the search, particularly the object identified by the warrant as the potential murder weapon and articles of clothing, all of them taken from my client's apartment."

The court reporter tapped away, recording my boilerplate.

"What exactly is the object you're talking about?" the judge asked.

"It's a marble obelisk," I said, "about a foot tall."

She jotted a note. "And the clothes?"

"Pants and a shirt," I said.

"Okay," she said. "Now what are the statements you allege are false, Mr. Rios?"

"Your Honor," I said, "the warrant was issued on the basis of an anonymous telephone call supposedly made by a tenant of the building where my client lived and received by the affiant, Detective McBeth. We intend to prove there was no such call, that, in fact, the description given by the putative caller of what he saw from where he saw it is physically impossible."

"I see," she said. "Let me take a look at the warrant." She opened her file and flipped through it. "Here it is. I'm going to take a minute to read it."

I heard the door to the courtroom open and looked back, hoping to see Holman. Instead, Bay Chandler quietly entered the room and took a seat at the back, near Harper. Her face tightened when she saw me. I turned my attention back to the judge.

When she finished reading the warrant, Torres-Jones said, "Will the People be calling any witnesses, Ms. Lang, or do you plan to stand on the warrant?"

Lang said, "The motion is frivolous, Your Honor. I'll submit on the warrant."

"All right, Mr. Rios," the judge said. "Call your first witness."

I said, "Your Honor, I'd like to call Detective McBeth under Evidence Code section seven seven six."

The judge looked over to the prosecution side of the table and asked, "You're Detective McBeth, I assume?"

"Yes, Your Honor."

"Mr. Rios is calling you as a hostile witness, Detective," she said. "But don't take the word hostile literally."

McBeth said, "I won't, Your Honor."

"All right, take the witness stand, Detective."

After McBeth was sworn, I went up to the lectern and began my questioning. I could see from the way she held herself and the tension in her face that she was expecting me to come out slugging. I smiled at her and in my friendliest tone said, "Good morning, Detective."

She smiled back and managed a pleasant, "Good morning."

"Detective, are you the investigating officer on this case?"

From behind me, Lang said, "The People will stipulate that Detective McBeth is the investigating officer."

"So stipulated," I said. "I hope everything goes this smoothly."

"Both of us, counsel," the judge said.

"Now, Detective McBeth, you began your investigation of Judge Chandler's murder on October eighth of this year, is that right?"

"Yes."

"And according to your affidavit, you received this anonymous call the same day?"

"That's right," she said.

"And this call directed you to my client's apartment, which you searched on the tenth, is that right?"

"Your Honor," Lang said, "that's all in the warrant."

"Counsel," the judge admonished, "in this court, you make objections, not observations. Answer the question, Detective."

"Yes, it did."

"Now isn't it true that LAPD was working on this case around the clock?"

"Yes."

"But other than this anonymous call, had your investigation developed any evidence connecting my client to Judge Chandler's murder?"

In her best police procedural monotone, she said, "I learned that your client was a beneficiary of the judge's will."

"And that was evidence that he might have killed the judge?"

"Objection, argumentative."

"No, I'll overrule it. Please answer."

"It was unusual because he wasn't a family member," McBeth said, "and he'd been added to the will only a couple of weeks before the judge was killed."

"Where did you get this information about the will?"

"From the Chandler family," she said.

"Who, specifically?" I pressed.

"Mrs. Chandler."

"Did Mrs. Chandler also tell you that she and the judge were separated because of Judge Chandler's romantic involvement with my client?"

"Yes, she told me that."

"And isn't it true that you considered my client's involvement with Judge Chandler to be evidence of my client's guilt?"

"No, I didn't," she replied.

I flipped through her affidavit. "Detective," I said, "isn't it true that on page five of your affidavit you stated, and I quote, 'the suspect had a homosexual relationship with the decedent' to show the anonymous tip you received was accurate?"

Lang got to her feet. "Objection, best evidence."

Torres-Jones said, "Overruled. Answer the question, Detective."

"Yes," she said.

"And what is it about a homosexual relationship that makes it likelier that someone will commit murder than a heterosexual relationship?" I asked.

"Objection, argumentative."

"Sustained," Torres-Jones said. "Anyway, you've made your point, Counsel. Ask another question."

"Did you also consider the other beneficiaries of Judge Chandler's will to be potential suspects?"

She glanced past me, at counsel table. Lang said, "Your Honor, I'm going to object on relevance grounds. This is completely peripheral to whether the warrant is valid."

Torres-Jones looked back and forth between us and said, "Counsel, approach the bench." We went up to the sidebar and she said, "Tell me where you're going with this, Mr. Rios."

"Judge, the validity of the search warrant depends completely on this witness's credibility. Why she chose to focus on my client as a suspect is relevant to the credibility issue."

"Your Honor," Lang said, "I see where Mr. Rios is going with this. He hopes to show that Detective McBeth is biased against homosexuals, but how is that relevant to the anonymous tip? It's not."

"Unless the tip was manufactured," I said.

Lang snorted. "That doesn't explain how the murder weapon or the bloody clothes got into the defendant's apartment."

"That does seem to be the problem with your motion," the judge said. "Unless you're suggesting that Detective McBeth planted the evidence."

"With all due respect, Your Honor," I said, "the question in this hearing isn't how the evidence came to be in my client's apartment, but whether Detective McBeth was being truthful about how she came to learn of it."

"Well, yes," the judge said, grudgingly. "I just don't see how you plan to answer the one question without getting into the other."

"Judge, the defense believes either that Detective McBeth lied in her affidavit about receiving a call or, if she did receive it, she failed to sufficiently corroborate it before she obtained the search warrant. Either her character is at issue or her competence is. I'm entitled to ask about both."

"That's ridiculous," Lang said. "Detective McBeth is not on trial here."

"Well, in a sense she is," the judge said, "because she did sign her name to the affidavit under penalty of perjury. Still, Mr. Rios, if it's the affidavit you're interested in, why don't you get to it?"

"I will," I said, "but I still think I'm entitled to probe McBeth's general credibility."

"I'll give you a few more minutes on this line of questioning," Torres-Jones said, "and then I'm going to cut you off."

"Thank you, judge," I said.

As Lang and I headed back to our respective places, I noticed that Karen Holman had finally arrived. Teddy was with her. I went back to the lectern and asked the reporter to reread my last question.

"No," McBeth said, "I didn't necessarily consider the other beneficiaries to be suspects."

"But that was enough to make you suspect my client," I said.

"Objection, argumentative."

"Sustained."

"Now, Detective McBeth, other than the will, what other evidence did you have that made you suspect my client?"

"I want to correct myself," she said. "I didn't necessarily consider your client a suspect because of the will, but I did want to talk to him. Unfortunately, he had disappeared."

"Well, let's talk about that, Detective. Why do you say he disappeared?"

"Well, he wasn't at his apartment and he didn't show up for work."

"Isn't it true that his apartment building had been evacuated because of the earthquake that occurred in the early morning hours of October eighth?"

"Yes," she said, "but the other tenants let the manager know where to reach them."

"But my client didn't, so you assumed he quote disappeared un-quote?"

"He also didn't show up for work."

"What was his job, Detective?"

"He worked as a waiter."

I smiled at her and said, "Not exactly skilled labor, is it?"

"Objection, Counsel is testifying."

"Sustained," Torres-Jones said, a note of impatience creeping into her voice. "All right, Mr. Rios, I think you need to ask about the affidavit."

"Yes, Your Honor, I appreciate the latitude you've given me so far."

She smirked as if doubting my sincerity and said, "You're quite welcome, now let's move on."

"Detective, do you have a copy of the search warrant with you?" I asked, politely.

"No, I don't."

"Your Honor, may I approach the witness?"

"Yes," the judge said.

At the witness box, I handed McBeth a copy of the warrant, turned to her affidavit. I'd underlined parts of it in pink highlighter. I stepped to the side of the box so that we could both read it. She tried to move away from me a bit, but the box confined her; seeing her discomfort, I moved closer.

"Now," I said, "looking at page two of the warrant, paragraph one, you identify the anonymous caller as a male. You're sure of that?"

"Yes, it was a male," she said.

"And according to your affidavit, he identified himself as a resident of the apartment complex where my client lived, right?"

"Yes," she said.

"And he lived on the second floor?"

"Yes," she said.

"And you're positive that's what he said?"

"Yes," she replied, casting a sideways glance at me.

"And," I said, moving closer still, until my breath creased her cheek, "your anonymous male caller said he saw my client pass in front of the kitchen window of his second-floor apartment as he was seated at the kitchen table, right?"

She flinched and said, "Do you have to stand so close?"

"Oh, I'm sorry, Detective," I said, stepping away. "Is that better?"

"Your Honor," Lang said, "Counsel is harassing the witness."

"Just answer the question, Detective," Torres-Jones said.

"Yes," McBeth said, "that's what he said."

"And you're sure about that?"

"Yes," she said.

"Now, Detective, you also say that after you received this call, you interviewed some of the tenants of the apartment building, right?"

"That's right, Counsel."

"Did you interview all the tenants?"

"No," she said. "I got the names and phone numbers of as many of the tenants as I could from the manager, Ms. Holman, and interviewed them."

"Did you ask specifically for the second-floor tenants or just make a general request?"

"I asked her for everyone she had numbers for."

"I see," I said. "And where did these interviews take place?"

"Over the phone," she said.

"Did you interview anyone at the apartment building itself?"

"No, it had been evacuated."

"And how did you reach Ms. Holman?"

"I located the owner of the building through the assessor's rolls and he put me in touch with Ms. Holman."

"So, prior to conducting the search, you never actually went to the apartment building, is that right?"

She hesitated, just for a second. "That's right."

"Wasn't it important to see the layout of the building to determine if it matched the anonymous caller's story of how he'd come to see my client?" I asked, wondering about that slight hesitation.

"I was concerned that the evidence might be removed, so I had to act quickly," she said. "There wasn't time to see the building."

It was plausible, but didn't explain that split-second pause, so I decided to work it a bit. "So your testimony is that the first time you went to the apartment building was on October tenth, when you carried out the search?"

"That's right," she said, more confidently.

"So you had no idea of whether there was even a second story on the building?"

"I confirmed that with the manager," she replied.

"I see," I said. I'd worked my way back to the lectern, and now I shuffled through some papers to buy a moment to think about what might have discombobulated her when I asked whether she'd been to the building before the search, but nothing obvious came to mind, so I asked, "Were you able to interview all the tenants whose phone numbers you got from Ms. Holman?"

"No," she said, "not all of them."

"Did you talk to Don Ward?"

"I'd have to look at my notes," she said.

"What about Ben Harper?"

"Harper, that name's familiar, but I'd have to look at my notes," she said.

"Darlene Sawyer?"

"Again, Counsel, I'd have to look at my notes."

"Do you have your notes with you, Detective?"

She smiled faintly as she said, "No, I don't."

"But you can obtain them?"

"I'd be happy to," she said.

"When you talked to the tenants, did you ask them whether they had made the anonymous call to you?"

"No," she said, "I was more indirect. I asked them general questions about what they might have seen the night of the murder."

"Why did you do that?"

"I wanted to see if I could identify the voice before I asked them about the call."

"I see," I said. "Was there anything particularly distinctive about the caller's voice that you thought would help you identify it if you heard it again?"

"I have a good ear," she said. "I was pretty sure I'd be able to identify it."

"And did any of the tenants you talked to match the voice of your anonymous caller?"

"No," she said.

Before court had begun, I'd had the bailiff bring an easel into the courtroom, where I'd propped up blowups of photographs of the apartment building. Now I directed McBeth's attention to the first photograph, which showed the second floor, looking toward Zack's apartment from the east stairwell.

"Do you recognize the building in this photograph, Detective?"

She took her time before answering. "Yes, it looks like the second floor of the defendant's apartment complex."

"Could you approach the photograph and identify my client's apartment in this photograph?"

She stepped down from the witness stand and again took her time as she studied the photograph. "There," she said, pointing to Zack's apartment at the end of the hall.

I handed her a black marker. "Could you mark it with an X, please?"

After she marked it, she looked at me. I smiled and said, "Nothing more of this witness at the moment, Your Honor."

"Ms. Lang, do you wish to examine the witness?"

"I have just a few questions," the D.A. said.

Her questions carried us past noon. She gave McBeth ample opportunity to expand her claim that she was concerned about the removal or destruction of the evidence as the reason she had conducted an abbreviated investigation to determine the anonymous caller's identity. It was the usual cop boilerplate to explain away shoddy work and Torres-Jones seemed unimpressed by it, but even if she found that McBeth should've done more to corroborate the tip, police negligence was not a ground to invalidate the warrant.

Just as the session ended, my pager went off. Freeman Vidor was trying to reach me. I had my witnesses ordered back and then ducked them, as I rushed to find a phone to return his call.

22

"YOU WERE RIGHT," FREEMAN SAID. I WAS AT A PHONE BOOTH IN the hall outside the courtroom. Darlene Sawyer drifted by and waved, followed by Ben Harper, who glared angrily at me for having had him ordered back. I turned away from him.

"Right about what?"

"The judge had dinner at the Epicenter the night he was killed," Freeman said. "It's that restaurant on Second Street in that Japanese hotel. The waiter remembered him because he had a lot of drinks while he was waiting for the guy he ate with."

I felt a surge of excitement. "Does he remember who Chris's dinner companion was?"

"Yeah," Freeman said. "It was some young kid. The waiter says they got into an argument and the kid left without ordering."

"What were they arguing about?"

"He wasn't close enough to hear," Freeman replied. "But the kid knocked his chair over getting up."

"What time was it?"

"Waiter says it was halfway through his shift. About eight, eight-thirty."

"Can he describe the boy?" I asked him.

"That's the best part," Freeman replied. "Said the kid was a pumped-up, littler version of the judge."

"Joey," I said. "I want to talk to this waiter tonight. Set up a meeting, would you?"

"How's the hearing going?"

"It's early yet," I said. "Call me later."

"Will do," Freeman said, and hung up.

My guess about Chris having eaten dinner with someone the night he was killed was based on the medical examiner's report that indicated he had eaten shortly before he died and consumed enough alcohol to get him drunk. Based on those facts, it was a reasonable guess, but just as likely wrong as right. So much of my work was looking down blind alleys, that when a hunch actually paid off, it gave me a rush. Now my thoughts were coming so fast, they spilled over each other. I had no doubt that it was Joey who'd met Chris for dinner that night. This, in turn, explained why Kimball hadn't laughed me out of his office the day before and even why Bay had showed up at the suppression hearing. The next step would be to talk to the waiter, then start issuing subpoenas. On my way to grab something to eat, I had to remind myself to slow down. There was still the suppression hearing to get through.

The D.A. was clearly worried that my strategy was to show McBeth had done an insufficient corroboration of the anonymous call before she rushed off to get a search warrant. It suited my purposes for her to think so. Pinning McBeth down to her statements in the affidavit was only the first step in my plan to impeach her credibility about the anonymous call. When court resumed I would call the second-floor tenants, one by one, to testify that none of them had made that call. Then I would call Karen Holman to testify to the physical layout of the building, by which I intended to establish that the only tenants who could've have seen Zack in the manner described by the anonymous caller were those tenants. Finally, I would call McBeth back to the stand to confront her with having lied to me at Midtown Hospital about going there to see a nonexistent friend when, in fact, she'd been following me to find Zack. I would argue to Torres-Jones that McBeth had targeted Zack from the outset of the investigation and, impatient to nail him, fabricated the anonymous call to get into his apartment to look for incriminating evidence.

I thought it was a good plan, though, of course, I'd also considered the counterarguments. Lang would argue that the anonymous caller could've lied about where he was when he saw Zack to protect himself from being identified, or even that one of my witnesses was lying about having made the call. She would object to the Midtown testimony as irrelevant or pass it off as standard police investigatory tactics. Above all, she would emphasize that McBeth had, in fact, found the evidence which the anonymous caller had told her she would find. That was the rub. I wasn't prepared to prove that McBeth had planted the evidence, because I couldn't, so the question remained, how could she have fabricated the call if she didn't know what she would find in advance of the search?

After lunch, Karen Holman waylaid me outside the courtroom and said, "Henry, Teddy has something to tell you." The boy sat on a bench, gravely investigating the gang signs that had been carved on it. "Teddy, come over here and tell Mr. Rios what you told me at lunch."

He hopped off the bench, hiked up jeans that were at least three sizes too big for him and came over.

"Make it quick," I told him. "We have to be back in court."

Then he told me, and I understood McBeth's brief hesitation when I'd asked her about when she'd first gone to the apartment building.

Back in court, I put on my witnesses as planned, save McBeth. Lang finished her cross-examination of Karen Holman, and Torres-Jones asked, wearily, "Any more witnesses, Mr. Rios?"

It was sometimes easier to read the future from the entrails of a cat than get a fix on what a judge was thinking, and Torres-Jones was particularly hard to get a handle on. Unlike many judges who felt their dignity required taciturn, stony neutrality, Torres-Jones was chatty and sardonic. She'd clearly liked Darlene Sawyer, who was as breezy in the witness box as she'd been in her friend's plant-filled living room, and she'd just as plainly disliked Ben Harper, whose sullen "huh-uhs" and "uh-uhs" had evoked from her schoolmarmish admonitions to answer yes or no for the court reporter's benefit. But except for the occasional questioning glance she cast in McBeth's direction, I couldn't tell whether she was following the thread of the testimony or, if so, whether it was convincing her. The only thing that was clear as the big court clock approached five was that she was tired.

"Just one more," I said.

"I'd like to finish this today and move on the prelim," she said.

"I don't think we can, Your Honor," I said. "I have this one witness, and then I'll probably be calling Detective McBeth back to the stand."

Almost inaudibly, the judge sighed. "All right, proceed."

"The defense calls Teddy Holman," I said.

She watched him approach the witness stand with baffled amusement and looked at me as if to say, What is this all about? I smiled and began. "Teddy, how old are you?"

"Ten and a half," he said, in a petrified voice.

"You nervous?"

I could see the "duh" in his eyes, but he managed a grown-up "Yes, sir."

"Just relax and tell the truth, okay."

"Your Honor," Lang said, "I object to this coaching."

Torres-Jones said, "Instructing a witness to be truthful is hardly coaching, counsel. Overruled."

"Teddy, do you know the difference between a lie and the truth?" I asked. It was a standard question for child witnesses.

"Yes, sir," he said.

I plucked at my red tie and said, "If I were to tell you that my tie is green, would I be telling the truth?"

He shook his head.

"You have to answer yes or no, Teddy," the judge said, with considerably more patience than she'd shown Ben Harper.

"No, your tie is red."

"Okay, do you remember the earthquake a few weeks back?"

"Yes, sir."

"And do you know the date of the earthquake?"

He started to shake his head, caught himself and said, "No."

"Your Honor," I said, "will the court take judicial notice that the earthquake occurred in the early morning hours of October eighth?"

"Judicial notice is taken," she said.

Teddy had listened uncomprehendingly to this exchange.

"I want you to assume the earthquake took place on October eighth, okay, Teddy."

"All right," he said, a little skeptically.

"Now, did you and your mother have to leave your apartment after the earthquake?"

Lang got to her feet. "Objection, leading the witness."

"It's permitted with a child witness," I said.

"Overruled," Torres-Jones said, "but don't put words in his mouth, Mr. Rios."

"Can you answer my question, Teddy? Did you and your mother leave your apartment?"

"Yeah, we had to stay in the park."

"And how far was the park from the apartment building?"

"It was two blocks," he said. "We stayed in a tent."

"And do you remember how many days you stayed in the tent?"

He counted on his fingers. "Two days," he said.

"Two days total, right?"

He nodded.

"So you moved back to your apartment on October tenth, is that right?"

He looked at me, his lips moving as he did the addition. "Yeah."

"Okay, Teddy, now between the time you moved out of your apartment on the eighth and the time you moved back to your apartment on the tenth, did you ever go back to the building?"

"Yes, sir."

"Okay, now what day was that? Can you figure that out?"

"It was the day after the earthquake," he said.

"That would have been October ninth," I said. "Do you remember what day it was?"

"It was Sunday," he said. "I remember 'cause I didn't have to go to school."

"Was your mother with you?"

He looked for her before answering. She must have nodded encouragement, because he answered loudly, "No."

"Did you tell her you were going to the building?"

"No, sir."

"And why didn't you tell her?"

"I didn't want to get in trouble."

"Why did you think you'd get in trouble?"

"She said the building wasn't safe and I should stay away from it until it was safe again."

"So why did you go back, Teddy?"

The question flustered him into silence.

"Teddy," I said, "she already knows, so you're not going to get into any more trouble if you tell the judge."

Torres-Jones added, "That's right, Teddy. Discipline is up to your mom, not me."

"I left my Gameboy," he said.

"Your Honor, for the record a Gameboy is—"

The judge cut me off, saying dryly, "I know what a Gameboy is, Mr. Rios. My husband's addicted to his."

"Pardon me," I said. "I didn't know what it was."

"You'd do well to keep it that way," she replied.

"I went just before my mom got home from work," Teddy told the judge.

"Objection," Lang said, "no question pending."

"Overruled," Torres-Jones said, beaming at the boy. "I think we can consider it an admission against Teddy's judicial interests."

I continued. "So what time would that have been?"

"Hmm, on Sundays she gets home at around five."

"Was it dark when you got to the building?"

"It was getting there," he said.

"At this point, Your Honor," I said, "I'd ask the court to take judicial notice that the day after October eighth, when Teddy said he left his apartment, would've been October ninth, the day before Detective McBeth testified she searched my client's apartment."

Lang got up. "Object to this testimony by counsel."

"No," Torres-Jones said, looking at me curiously, then at Teddy. "He's only relaying what's already in evidence. I will take judicial notice that the date in question was October ninth."

I turned my attention back to Teddy. "Okay," I said, "what did you do when you got to your apartment?"

"I went inside and got my Gameboy."

"And then what did you do?"

"I tried to watch TV, but the power wasn't on," he said. "Then I started cleaning stuff up."

"While you were in your apartment, did you hear anything?"

"Yes, sir."

"What did you hear?"

"I heard someone outside."

"What exactly did you hear?"

"Um, someone walking around? Going up the stairs?"

"And what did you do when you heard the footsteps?"

"I got scared," he said.

"Why were you scared?"

"I thought it was looters."

"So what did you do then?" I asked him.

"I went to see who it was," he said.

"Why did you do that?"

" 'Cause, my mom's the manager and if there was looters, she might lose her job and I wanted to see who it was so I could tell her and she could tell the police."

"That was a brave thing to do," the judge commented.

The compliment puffed him up, and whatever remaining nervousness he felt about being on the stand seemed to leave him.

"What did you do?" I asked.

"I went up the stairs and I looked to see who it was."

"And when you did that, were you standing in the hallway?"

He shook his head. "I was, like, behind the wall."

"But you could see down the hallway, right?"

"Uh-huh. I mean, yes."

I referred him to the photograph of the second floor I'd introduced during McBeth's testimony.

"Okay, Teddy," I said, "I want you to go to the picture and point out where you were standing."

He left the stand, approached the picture and pointed to the wall that framed the doorway at the top of the stairs on the east end of the second floor.

"So you were more or less peeking out from behind that wall, right?"

"Yes, sir," he said.

"You can sit down again." After he returned to the witness stand, I asked, "Now, Teddy, did you see anyone in the hall?"

"Not right away," he said.

"Did you see anyone at any time while you were standing there?"

"Yes, sir," he said, the nervousness returning.

"Is that person in court today?"

He looked around, panic in his eyes.

"Teddy?" I said gently.

"I saw her," he blurted, pointing at McBeth.

"For the record," I said, "the witness has identified Detective Mc-Beth."

"Noted," the judge said, wonder in her tone.

"Where did you see Detective McBeth?" I asked.

Lang got to her feet. "Your Honor, I'd like to approach the bench."

Torres-Jones glared at her. "Denied. Where did you see her, Teddy?"

"Um, she was coming out of Zack's apartment," he said, looking away from her and back to me, his eyes appealing for approval.

I nodded. "You mean Zack Bowen, the man sitting behind me?"

"Yes, sir."

"And how did you know it was Zack's apartment?"

"I go there after school sometimes, when my mom's not home, and we watch TV until she comes to get me."

"And you're sure Detective McBeth was coming out of his apartment?"

"Yes, sir."

"And you're sure it was Detective McBeth?"

"Yes, sir."

"Had you ever seen her before?"

"No, sir."

"And have you seen her since that day?"

"Right now," he said.

"You mean in the courtroom today?"

"Yes, sir."

"And when she came out of Zack's apartment, was she carrying anything with her?"

"No, sir," he said.

"And what did you do when you saw her?"

"I ran downstairs back to my apartment."

"And how long did you stay there?"

"Until I heard her go."

"Okay," I said, "just to make sure. This happened the day after the earthquake, right?"

He paused, thought it over, and said, "Yes, sir."

"Just a couple more questions, Teddy. Are you friends with Zack?" I asked him.

Teddy reddened a bit. "He's okay," he said, tepidly.

I knew from talking to Karen Holman that Teddy liked Zack but was embarrassed because he knew Zack was gay. Even at his age, he had that pegged as a shameful thing. I thought about bringing this out to support his credibility, but decided it would only embarrass the boy further and hurt Zack's feelings.

"You understand that the police say Zack killed someone?"

"Yeah," he mumbled, looking down.

"Would you lie for Zack to help him out?"

He sank into the chair and said, "No, sir."

"And is everything you've told the judge the truth?"

He managed a final, "Yes, sir."

"No further questions," I said.

•   •   •

The courtroom was absolutely still.

"Ms. Lang," the judge said. "Do you have any questions for this witness?"

"We didn't expect this, Your Honor," she said without affect. "I'd prefer to reserve my cross-examination until tomorrow morning."

Torres-Jones said, "Yes. The witness is ordered back at nine o'clock." She scanned the audience. "If there are any problems with his school, Ms. Holman, my clerk will call. Court stands in recess."

After she left the bench, I went to the witness box and walked Teddy to his mother. Lang and McBeth were in furious, whispered conversation. As I explained to Teddy that he would have to return the next morning, Bay Chandler brushed by me. When I returned to counsel table to say good-night to Zack before he was returned to the jail, I saw her standing behind the D.A. She saw me, smiled faintly and looked away.

When I left the court, she was deep in conversation with Lang in a corner of the courtroom, while McBeth remained at counsel table, shuffling the same papers over and over.

23

AT EIGHT-THIRTY THE NEXT MORNING, LANG STOPPED ME IN THE
hall outside the courtroom with a brusque, "We need to talk."

I saw the fatigue etched into her pale face and decided not to take it
personally. "Sure. Here?"

"The jury room," she replied.

The jury room was a monastic box dominated by a big table, plain,
uncomfortable chairs and a No Smoking sign. We sat across from each
other. I offered her the paper cup of coffee I'd brought from the cafeteria.

"No, thanks," she said. "Mind if I smoke?"

"Your lungs," I said.

She lit up with a grimace, tossing the spent match on the floor and
said, "I've been authorized by the D.A. to offer you a deal."

"I'm not interested in a plea bargain."

She batted smoke from her face and replied irritably, "Not that kind
of deal. Hear me out."

"Go ahead."

She dragged on the cigarette and spoke through a mouthful of
smoke. "If you withdraw your suppression motion, I'll dismiss the
charges for insufficient evidence and we'll both walk away from this
disaster."

In twenty years of practice, I had never heard anything like this. I
wasn't even sure it could be done, and said as much.

"Of course it can be done," she said. "You get up and withdraw your motion and then I get up and say the People have decided to dismiss the complaint on the grounds that there's not enough evidence against your guy to go to trial. What's hard about that?"

"If I withdrew my motion," I pointed out, "there would be enough evidence to go to trial."

She crushed her cigarette on the floor. "Don't be an asshole, Henry, you know what this is about."

"I'm afraid I don't."

She tipped her head back, sighed and said, "The bitch lied to me and perjured herself on the stand." She looked at me. "Don't tell me you didn't know. I'm tough, Henry, but I don't suborn perjury. You could've told me and I would have taken care of it."

"This deal," I said, the truth slowly dawning on me. "It's to protect her. Why?"

"It's not my decision," she said, wearily. "If it was up to me, I'd throw her to the dogs, but she's the first black woman to make it to detective two in Homicide. It sets a bad precedent if she ends up being indicted for perjury."

"So she gets to walk away from it? Is that fair?"

"She's not walking away from it," Lang said. "She'll be canned, but it'll be done administratively."

"Behind closed doors."

"She's going to lose her job. Isn't that enough? What do you want, a pound of flesh?"

I got up and walked to the window. It was overcast, with the threat of rain looming the dank November air. First Street was jammed with morning commuters. I thought about Zack sitting in his windowless cell. Lang was right; what happened to McBeth was not the point. My responsibility was to my client. All I had to do was say yes, and he'd be back home by nightfall. But not innocent. Even dismissed, the charge would hang over his head for the rest of his life, and the cops could reopen the investigation at any time, since there is no statute of limitations on murder.

"I'll take the deal if you'll stipulate there's a factual basis to dismiss the charge."

It took a moment for it to sink in. Then she sputtered, "What! You want me to go on the record and say he's innocent?"

"We haven't started the trial," I said. "Jeopardy hasn't attached. You could keep hauling him into court for the rest of his life."

"But he did it," she said.

"For what it's worth, I don't think he did," I replied. "But regardless, I don't want you going after him again."

"That's better than he'd get if you won the damn motion," she said. "That's the deal."

She got up. "I have to talk to some people, but for the record, I'll advise against it because it's bullshit. He killed a Superior Court judge. That's death penalty territory. I'd take the damn thing to trial with nothing before I agreed to let him walk."

"Apparently, that's not your decision to make," I said.

"I'll see you in court," she replied, and stormed out of the room.

Fifteen minutes later, she was back in the courtroom, just as Torres-Jones was about to take the bench. She was not alone. There was a serious suit with her, pallid and gray-haired, hatchet man written all over him. I recognized him as William Goar, second-in-command in the D.A.'s office, a lifer who'd already outlasted half a dozen D.A.s. He walked over to me.

"Counsel," he said, extending his hand perfunctorily.

"Do we have a deal?" I asked him, ignoring it.

"Two conditions," he said. "We do it in chambers and you agree not to make any statements to the press."

"Agreed," I said.

"Fine," he replied, and walked away.

The bailiff announced the judge. She did a double-take when she saw Goar, then settled in her chair and called the case.

"William Goar for the People, Your Honor," Goar said. "May we approach the bench?"

"Yes," she said. He made her nervous. I couldn't blame her, he only lacked a scythe to be the Dark Angel himself.

"Your Honor," he said, "we've agreed to a disposition of this case, but we'd prefer to discuss the terms in chambers."

"With the reporter," I chimed in.

"Of course," Goar said.

"Are you going to give me a hint?" she asked, irritably.

"Dismissal," he said, flatly.

"Give me five minutes, then come back," she said.

While we waited, I explained to Zack what was about to happen, but it was too much for him to take in, and I left him with a confused expression on his face when I followed Goar and Lang back to chambers, the reporter trailing along with her machine.

Torres-Jones's chambers had a lived-in look, pictures on the walls, a colorful area rug covering the fecal brown carpeting beneath it, a coffee machine and a collection of mugs on the credenza, a vase filled with yellow roses on the corner of her desk. Out of her robe, in a brown pants suit and flat shoes, she looked more like the president of the PTA than a judge. She offered us coffee. We all politely declined.

"Well, what's the deal?" she asked.

"This part doesn't need to be on the record," Goar instructed the reporter, whose hands hovered just above the keys of her machine. Torres-Jones cast a sour look in his direction, but said nothing. "The deal is, counsel here withdraws his motion and we ask for a dismissal in the interests of justice."

"After stipulating that a factual basis exists for it," I reminded him.

"Yeah," he said. "We do that part back here, then you dismiss the case in open court."

"Are you serious?" she asked.

"This comes from the District Attorney himself," Goar said.

"What makes you think I'd go along with something like that?" she demanded. "It's totally irregular."

Goar grimaced. "These are standard motions."

"It's a backroom deal," she said. "Look, why don't we do it the right way? I'm going to grant the motion to suppress—I don't see what else I can do after yesterday—and then we proceed to the prelim."

"If you grant the motion," Goar said, "we can't proceed on the pre-lim."

"Fine," she said, "then I won't bind the defendant over and the charge is dismissed."

"There are certain problems with that," Goar said quietly.

"Like what, Mr. Goar?"

"Let's start with yours," he said, just as quietly. "You become the judge who suppressed evidence in a high-profile murder case. The police department will have to contend with an officer who perjured herself and the District Attorney will come out looking like he sub-orned it."

Clearly taken aback, Torres-Jones stared at him without speaking.

"Your Honor," I said, "I realize this is unusual, but the defense is willing to go along."

"Of course you are," Goar said crisply. "That's not the point. The point is the criminal justice system in this city has taken enough hits in the last ten years without all of us going out there and admitting that we fucked up again. The D.A. wants this done as quietly as possible."

"And what about Detective McBeth?" the judge demanded.

"She will be dealt with," Goar replied.

"If you stipulate to a factual basis for the dismissal," Torres-Jones said, "you're stopped from ever charging the defendant again."

"We understand that," Goar said.

"And that's all right with you?" she said incredulously. "They found the damned weapon in his apartment."

"Which evidence you are about to suppress," Goar pointed out.

For a moment, no one said anything, until the judge broke the silence. "When I dismiss the charge in open court," she said, "I'll make it clear I'm doing so at the request of the People."

"You can cover your ass any way you have to," Goar said.

"Counsel, I could hold you in contempt for that," she replied.

"My apologies to the court," he said, indifferently. "The People will stipulate that the dismissal is at their request. May we proceed?"

Torres-Jones glanced at the reporter. "We're on the record."

When we cut our deal in chambers, we all filed back out into the courtroom and waited for Torres-Jones to come out.

"Not a bad day's work for you," Goar said to me.

"Why did McBeth do it?" I asked him.

"Who cares?" he replied. "She's history."

Lang spoke for the first time since we'd talked in the jury room. "There was a call, but she didn't trust it, so she decided, just this once, to bend the rules."

"So she went into Zack's apartment, confirmed that the obelisk and the clothes were there, then wrote up her affidavit."

"That's right," she replied.

"What did Mrs. Chandler tell you yesterday afternoon?"

"About the key," she said.

"The key?"

"You didn't know? Oh, what the hell. It doesn't matter. She gave McBeth her husband's keys. One of them was to your guy's apartment. That's how McBeth got in."

"Bay knew about that?"

"No," Lang said. "McBeth told her she needed the keys for prints. After Mrs. Chandler heard the boy's testimony, she figured it out and felt she had to tell me."

"I see," I said.

The bailiff called us to order. Torres-Jones took the bench. "People versus Bowen," she said. "The defendant is presented in court and represented by counsel, Mr. Rios. The People are represented by Ms. Lang and Mr. Goar. Pursuant to our discussion in chambers, and at the People's request, the information is dismissed in the interests of justice. Mr. Goar?"

"The People stipulate that the dismissal is at their request."

"There was no bail set in this case," the judge said. "Therefore, the defendant is ordered to be released forthwith. The court stands in recess."

"What does that mean?" Zack whispered.

"It means you're free," I said.

He began to weep.

.   •   •

I had trouble sleeping that night.

The case was over. My client was free—back in his apartment, no doubt, picking up the shreds of his life. Yet I didn't feel the elation that usually came after I'd successfully defended a case. There were too many loose ends and they continued to drift in and out of my consciousness. One thing I was sure about. The way the case had ended would effectively close the investigation into Chris's murder, since the police would assume that Zack had killed him. No one would be going after Joey Chandler.

Zack free, Joey safe, everybody happy.

24

IT WAS TWO WEEKS BEFORE I COULD THINK ABOUT THE CASE AGAIN, because Josh went back into the hospital complaining of kidney pain. As had so often happened in the past, he had borne it stoically until it reached a critical stage and his kidneys were irretrievably damaged, but that was not the worst news. Dr. Singh had located the cause of the damage and asked me to be present when he talked to Josh. We were in the same room we had been in the last time he was hospitalized. Beneath the bed coverings, Josh was thinner and more frail than ever, hardly more than a stick figure. He was on a Demerol drip while another line carried antivirals into him, a third, liquid nutrition, and a fourth removed his wastes. His world had shrunk to the confines of his bed. He slept most of the time. When he was awake he was either drugged or in excruciating pain. For some reason his hands and feet were swollen and his skin was yellowish and rough. I scarcely recognized him, but the image of him wired to that bed kept me awake at night, night after night.

"Hello, love," I said, kissing his forehead. "How do you feel today?"

"Okay," he said.

His eyes were clearer than they'd been the day before, a sign that he was going easy on the Demerol.

"Singh said he wanted to talk to us," I said. "These flowers need fresh water."

I could feel his eyes following me as I took the vase of white roses from the bedstand and went into the bathroom to change the water. I avoided looking into the mirror, afraid of what I'd see on my face, fatigue, grief, confusion.

"Thank you," he said, when I returned. "They smell nice."

"Have your parents been in this morning?"

"Mom's coming later," he said. "My sisters are coming."

I nodded. His sisters lived in Sacramento and Denver. His mother had called them and told them to come say their good-byes.

"This is it," he said.

I sat down in a chair beside the bed and held his hand. Singh came in. Crisply, he took Josh's pulse, examined his vital signs and chatted with him about how he felt. Then he sat down at the edge of the bed and looked at both of us.

Without a preface, he said, "The damage to your kidneys is the result of the foscavir."

I ran through the various medications, trying to remember what foscavir was for, but Josh got there first.

"For my eyes," he said.

Singh nodded. "That's right, for the CMV. It has this effect on many patients," he said. "You've got to stop taking it intravenously."

"I'll go blind," Josh replied, quietly.

"No," Singh said, "there are a couple of other ways we can administer it. We could implant it or we could inject directly into your eyes, using a pediatric needle."

"Wait," I said. "You mean you'd stick a needle into his eyes?"

"It sounds barbaric," Singh said, "but it's not as bad as all that. Implants would be better. Either way, we get the drug to the source of the virus and minimize any further damage to his kidneys."

"Don't talk about me like I'm not here," Josh said.

"I'm sorry, Josh," Singh replied.

"What about the damage that's already been done?" I asked.

Singh launched into an explanation of what was required to keep Josh's kidneys from failing. He was in midsentence when Josh cut him.

"No more," he said, in the stubborn tone I recognized as his final word on any subject. "I want off all the drugs."

In the ensuing silence, the implication slowly crept up on me. His immune system was destroyed and he was fighting or vulnerable to any number of viruses or infections that, without the drugs, would ravage him. As if it was possible he could be ravaged any further.

Singh looked at me, questioningly.

"It's Josh's decision," I said.

"I want to go home," Josh said, the forcefulness gone from his voice. "To Henry's."

In his gentlest voice, Singh said, "You know without the drugs, you won't have much time."

"How much?" Josh rasped.

"Weeks," Singh replied. "Days."

Josh said, "I want this to be over."

He squeezed my hands and closed his eyes. In a few minutes, he was asleep.

"Come outside for a moment," Singh said. I got up and followed him to the hall. "Are you up to this, Henry?"

"Of course I am," I said, irritably. "What do you think, I'm going to let him die in here?"

He touched my arm and replied, "Excuse me for saying this, but you look terrible."

"I haven't been able to sleep," I said. "I'll sleep better if he's with me."

"He'll need full-time nursing."

"I'll arrange it," I said.

Singh nodded. "All right. Once we get him some nursing, I'll arrange his release. Actually, going off his meds may be a good idea at this point. He might even rally a bit once they work their way out of his system and you'll have him back for a while. But only for a while."

I closed my eyes against the tears and said, "I'll take whatever I can get."

So I brought him home. The days that followed were hectic, as I tried to adjust myself to the demands of his sickness, including the constant flow of people in and out of the house, nurses, his family, friends. As Singh predicted, once the extremely toxic drugs he was taking passed through his body, he regained some of his mental acuity and he even felt better physically than he had in a long time, though he remained very weak. Although it was now late November, the weather remained mild and he spent as much time as he could on the terrace. I brought my work outside and sat with him, or read to him or watched him as he dozed. Not that it was always so serene. He'd wake in the middle of the night, disoriented and frightened, and I'd have to calm him down. Or he'd stumble out of bed and fall and wake me with his cries. There were days when the pain was so intense he'd lash out at me or threaten to kill himself, after all, and other days when he was rendered mute by depression. As for me, I realized I was not as prepared as I thought for his death; that at some level, I did not believe he would really die. Now, the actuality of it washed over me like a cold wave and left me numb with shock.

One morning, we were sitting on the terrace, and he said, "What really happened to your friend, the judge?"

"Chris Chandler?" I hadn't thought about the case in weeks.

He pulled an old, bulky sweater around him. "You got that guy off. Zack? If he didn't kill him, who did?"

"I can't prove it, but I think it was his son."

"His son," Josh repeated. "His own son killed him because he was a fag. Why do you think they hate us so much, Henry?"

"I don't know," I said. "I don't think I'll ever know."

"The worst thing about it is you start to think maybe they're right to hate you."

"You don't believe that, do you?"

He frowned. "The guy who infected me wasn't some crazy fundie, Henry. He was another fag."

"It wasn't intentional," I said.

"How do you know?" he replied. "Maybe he knew he was HIV when we had sex, but he figured we deserved it for being queer."

"That may happen," I conceded, "but I'd like to think it's rare."

"Maybe, but you have to admit gay men can treat each other with as much contempt as straights do."

"Who do you think we learned it from," I said. "There's a line from a poem by Auden, 'Those to whom evil is done/Do evil in return.' We're not immune. It takes incredible strength to withstand hatred without internalizing some of it."

"Or acting it out," Josh said.

"Why are you thinking about this?"

He looked out to the canyon, gathering his thoughts. "I'm dying," he said, "and the man who's responsible for it was also gay. I'm not saying I'm not responsible, too," he added quickly. "But the bottom line is another gay man did this to me."

"What about the gay man who loves you," I said.

He looked at me tenderly. "That's what's keeping me alive."

A couple of days later, I had to go to court for a hearing in an old case of mine on which the Court of Appeals had reversed the sentence because the trial judge had made a technical error the first time around. It took the judge ten minutes to correct his mistake and resentence my client to exactly the same term. On my way out of the courtroom, I saw Yolanda McBeth sitting by herself in the back row. I glanced away and kept walking, but halfway to the elevator, I heard her call my name. I stopped, turned and waited for her to catch up with me.

With a faint smile, she said, "You could at least have said hello."

"Did you really want me to? What are you doing here?"

"I'm still a cop," she said. "Suspended without pay until they figure out what to do with me. Meanwhile, I still have to show up on my cases, not that I'm worth much as a witness since word got around about what you did to me."

"You did it to yourself," I said.

"Look, Mr. Rios, I don't want to fight with you. I just wanted to talk. You never did hear my side."

"Does it matter? The case is closed."

"It matters to me," she said, a fierceness in her eyes. "I worked damn hard to get where I am and I did it by the rules until this one time. I want you to know why."

I gestured to a bench. "Okay, let's sit down and talk."

She smiled again. "It bothers you, doesn't it?"

"What?" I asked, as we sat down.

"The case. The judge was a friend of yours, so was his wife. It bothers you that you got his killer off."

"Zack didn't do it," I said.

"The weapon was in his apartment, Mr. Rios."

"Maybe you put it there," I said.

"Even you don't believe that," she said. "You read the police reports. The weapon was gone before I even got to the crime scene. What I wanted to tell you is that there was a call."

Now it was my turn to show disgust. "Come on, Detective."

"Hear me out," she said. "There was a call. A man. He phoned the day after the murder and described in detail the weapon and the bloody clothes and told me exactly where I'd find them. The problem was, he wouldn't give me any identification at all. I knew I couldn't get a warrant on that kind of tip because there was no way to corroborate it."

"So you got Chris's keys from Bay and did a little sleuthing off the books?"

"Whatever," she said. "Yeah, I got the keys and went to take a look and I found the weapon and the clothes where he said they would be. So I went back to the station and wrote up my affidavit. I did a shitty job, obviously, but the fact is, there was a call."

"Why should I believe you?"

"Because like you said, Mr. Rios, the case is closed, and there's no reason for me to lie. Besides, there was another call, too. Same caller."

"And he told you what?" I asked, intrigued in spite of my reluctance to believe her.

"That Bowen was up in the cabin."

"That's not true," I said, quickly. "You had me followed up there."

She looked at me as if I was speaking Finnish. "What are you talking about?"

"I know you followed me to Midtown Hospital, hoping I'd lead you to Zack," I said, getting angry at being taken for a fool. "And then you had me tailed up to the cabin by the San Bernardino sheriff's department."

She shook her head. "The hospital, yeah, I followed you," she said, "because I figured you were lying about whether you'd seen Bowen, but I didn't know anything about the cabin. I certainly didn't have you followed by the San Bernardino sheriffs."

"I was stopped on the way to the cabin by a sheriff who was with you when you arrested Zack."

"So what?" she replied. "I was operating in their jurisdiction, so I had to tell them what I was up to and they sent along some officers. I didn't choose them. Why don't you want to believe this?"

Because you're a liar, I wanted to say, but even as the words formed in my head, I knew that wasn't the reason, not completely, anyway. If what she was saying was true, it threatened to upset my theory that Joey Chandler killed his father, because I couldn't see how Joey would've known that Zack was in the cabin.

I still distrusted McBeth too much to reveal this to her, so I said, "So who do you think your mystery caller was?"

"Bowen's accomplice," she said.

The thought chilled me, but I wasn't about to give her the satisfaction of letting on, so I said, "What accomplice?"

"The judge left Bowen half a million dollars in his will," she said. "He found out and wanted it, so he talked someone into helping him do the judge, then got greedy and reneged. The second guy decided to get back at him by turning him in, but he didn't want to get himself arrested in the process, so he made the anonymous calls."

"There was no evidence of a second killer," I said.

"There was damn little evidence of anything," she pointed out. "Maybe the guy was a lookout, or maybe he was supposed to alibi Bowen. Maybe he came in afterwards and helped him clean up. I don't know that part, but take my word, Henry, there were two of them."

I got up. "That's all very interesting, but I don't believe it."

She narrowed her eyes, assessingly, and said, "You really think Bowen's innocent, don't you?"

"Zack loved Chris. That's the part you've never understood, Detective, because you're too blinded by your prejudices."

"Oh, so now I'm a bigot," she said. "Maybe you haven't noticed that I'm black. I know all about prejudice."

"That's too easy," I replied.

"Believe what you want, Henry, but I didn't go after your guy because he was gay. I went after him because he's guilty."

Later, I called the San Bernardino sheriff's department. I spoke to the officer who'd represented the department the night Zack was arrested and he said, no, they had not been working with LAPD to conduct a surveillance of me, and had never heard of McBeth or her investigation until that night.

25

I WAS FAR FROM CONVINCED BY MCBETH'S SCENARIO, BUT I KEPT returning to it as I thought over what I knew about the case. Josh, sensing my preoccupation, drew the story out of me as we sat on the terrace in the mornings before I went into my office to work. It was a good diversion for both of us, and as we talked it over, I had to admit that as a hypothetical, McBeth's version had a lot going for it.

Her notion that Zack had an accomplice, for instance, explained Sam Bligh, someone whose interest in Zack I had never entirely believed was purely sentimental. But suppose instead that Zack learned of the bequest and shared the information with Bligh. They conspired to kill Chris and split the money. That explained why Bligh sheltered him after the murder, but then Bligh began to suspect Zack was going to double-cross him. He sent Zack packing to the cabin, then made the anonymous calls leading to his arrest. Of course, he didn't actually want Zack to be convicted of the crime, because the will could be successfully contested; he just wanted to teach him a lesson. Bligh was sophisticated enough to know that anonymous phone calls to the police would probably not hold up in court. Just to make sure, he hired me to defend Zack instead of throwing him to the mercy of the overworked Public Defender's office. Now that Zack was free of the charge, the will would be probated, he would collect his money, and Bligh could guarantee his split with the threat of blackmail.

But what if I hadn't got Zack off? Bligh would've wasted his money on my fee for nothing. Still, my fee was considerably less than the quarter-million he would get if I was successful, so maybe it was worth the risk to him. It was not hard for me to imagine Bligh making these calculations. His business was not for the sentimental or the faint of heart and he'd made it pay, handsomely. I was keenly aware I was operating out of my own prejudices here in making the jump from pornography to murder, but now was not the moment for political rectitude. Put another way: just because I suspected the worst of Bligh didn't mean he wasn't capable of it.

The problem in this scenario for me was Zack Bowen. McBeth assumed he had killed Chris for money, but if Zack had been after money, he could have exploited Chris's infatuation as the occasion to pick his pockets. He hadn't done that. Taking money from Chris would have seemed like a step backward to the streets where he'd prostituted himself as a boy. I thought of his lovingly decorated little apartment and the sliver of self-respect it represented. That seemed infinitely more important to him than money.

The only remotely tenable reason Zack might have killed Chris was that Chris was going to leave him. Plainly, he was haunted by the possibility; it was the reason he thought Chris wanted to see him the night Chris was killed. It wasn't an entirely unreasonable fear. Chris kept secrets. Maybe he was planning to dump Zack and Zack picked up on it. Maybe Bligh fed that fear for his own purposes, convincing Zack of the injustice of Chris's treatment of him until he exploded in rage. I remembered the conversation I'd had with Josh just a couple of days earlier about how gay men acted out their self-hatred on each other. Their fears, too. And yet it was hard for me to put Zack in that room, battering Chris's brains out.

No, not Zack.

Then who?

Joey Chandler?

That scenario still held its attractions for me. Joey had quarreled with Chris at dinner hours before Chris was killed. Maybe, Joey left the restaurant in a rage, then followed his father back to the court where he continued their argument about Chris's abandonment of his family. Or Zack and a life toward which Joey felt contempt and hatred. In the heat of the quarrel, Joey killed his father, then panicked and left. Later, he realized he had left his prints on the obelisk and re-turned for it. That's when Zack saw him. Zack didn't recognize Joey, but Joey must've recognized Zack. It gave him the idea of planting the obelisk in Zack's apartment, then calling McBeth.

What about the second call to McBeth? How could Joey have known Zack was at Bligh's cabin? I struggled for a plausible explana-tion, but the best I could come up with is that Joey had been tailing Zack and followed him up to the cabin. Why would he have been tailing Zack? Maybe he was looking for an opportunity to plant further incriminating evidence on him. He might have realized that Zack's departure from the city was itself a suspicious circumstance.

There was no way of knowing if any of this was true, short of talking to Joey, but one other bit of hard evidence tended to support my theory. After I talked to Joseph Kimball, Bay showed up for the sup-pression hearing. Since she was not going to be called to testify by either side, I had concluded her reason for being there was to see whether I carried out my threat of implicating Joey. When McBeth's credibility fell apart, Bay provided the final nail in McBeth's coffin by disclosing to the D.A. that she had given Chris's keys to McBeth. As a result, the case against Zack was dismissed. To anyone other than Bay this would've been cause for alarm, because now the police might turn their attention to Joey. But Bay was a lawyer's daughter and a judge's wife. She would've understood that the dismissal was not an adjudica-tion of Zack's innocence or guilt, but a technical maneuver that left everyone still convinced that Zack was the killer. Thus, the case was closed and Joey protected. It seemed to me she wouldn't have gone to these lengths except to protect Joey which, as far as I was concerned, implied his guilt.

And yet, I had the same problem with Joey as murderer as I had with Zack; imagining the actual act of killing. Of course, sons killed their fathers, but even at his worst, Chris was hardly the kind of father who drives his children to parricide.

• • •

Ultimately, the problem with either scenario was not so much what it required me to think of Zack or Joey, but what it required me to think of Chris. He was a complicated mix, no doubt about it, decent but self-aggrandizing, courageous but also cowardly, a man who lived a lie for most of his life but managed admirable achievements nonetheless. I'd known him at every stage of his adult life, sometimes intimately while at other times there had been something akin to enmity between us. I'd loved him once when we were boys, had pitied him, been contemptuous of him and come to admire him again. He was for me, as I was for him, a kind of doppelganger, the ghostly reverse images of ourselves. No one could have felt more ambivalent about him than me, but even at my most disdainful I never doubted that at root Chris Chandler was a good man and a man who strove toward goodness. His idea of the good wasn't my idea, but it was one that I understood.

We obeyed different imperatives. Chris took the world as he found it and believed he could not make his mark on it without denying his sexual nature. It wasn't that he thought being gay was immoral or unnatural; he'd assured me of that from the start. Instead, I think he viewed it as a disadvantage he had to overcome to succeed, something on par with growing up poor. Nor was his idea of success a matter of crass materialism. He wanted a family, children, to be the kind of husband and father he wished his own father had been. Those were the wrongs he wanted to right, and they were far more urgent for him than sexual expression.

But that was where we disagreed. I couldn't equate being gay with sexual practices alone, because I was gay whether or not I was having sex, when sex was the last thing on my mind. It wasn't separate from who I was; it was part of who I was. Chris thought he could sacrifice a little pleasure for a stable place in the world, but to me the sacrifice would've been of the thing that made me human, the ability to love and to be loved, the drive toward connectedness. No position in the world was more important to me than that, because without it all positions would have been empty.

It wasn't that I thought these recognitions made me a better person than Chris. Certainly, in the judgment of the world, there was no comparison between his achievements and mine. He was a respected judge, a good husband, a loving father, while I was an alcoholic homosexual who defended criminals for a living. Over the years, I'd occasionally envied him his apparent happiness and wondered if I hadn't thrown away my own potential for happiness, but then I realized I could not have done other than I'd done because to do so, I'd have had to be a different person. Maybe I had taken the path of least resistance and Chris the more courageous course, and the success he'd reaped was a tribute to his virtue and not, as I had sometimes bitterly thought, rewards for his hypocrisy. Maybe he was right and I was wrong, if those words have any real application to the experience of living, but if I was wrong, it was not out of moral evil, or sickness or criminal disposition, that much I was sure of. I had followed my truth as I understood it, and if my life was a failure, it was because I had misunderstood.

But I didn't think my life was a failure. It was different from the lives of most people, and for that reason often more difficult than I observed their lives to be, but it was a life largely without regrets or fear. I knew I had done, was doing, the best I could. Chris, too, had done the best he could. Anyone who knew him knew that much. And anyone who knew that much about him would not have harmed him.

Not Zack.

Not Joey.

The person who had killed Chris was a stranger to him. With that premise in mind, I went over and over the facts of the case, with Josh and alone, but no conscious solution would come. And then, three days after I'd talked to McBeth, I woke up from a dream, the details of which evaporated as soon as the light touched my eyes but for a name that seemed both obvious and inexplicable. I reached the same conclusion when I applied the facts to it; everything fit except for a motive. I could see how he'd done it, but not why. So I called the one person who I was certain could supply the reason.

26

BLIGH'S LIVING ROOM WAS FILLED WITH FRESH-CUT FLOWERS, spilling their fragrance across the white spaces where the only sound was the occasional passing of a car on the street below. Courteous as ever, he poured me coffee and then settled into one of the elegant chairs. He'd been apprehensive on the phone when I insisted that I had to see him alone, but now he'd regained his composure and studied me with a polite expression, only the faintest trace of guardedness in his clear blue eyes. I took my time, looking around the room, cataloging the artifacts of his comfortable life. Their opulence had something to do with why I was there; he'd acquired a taste for opulence, but he wanted it on his own terms.

Greed had always seemed to me the most self-defeating of vices because one cannot own anything permanently; we have, at most, a life tenancy in our possessions. But I suppose the fulfillment was in the acquisition and maybe, too, someone who'd been tossed around by life needed the cosseting that money and things provide. Someone like him.

I'd spent the last two days learning all about him, with McBeth's help. She'd been distrustful at first, but as I spun my theory, her good cop instincts overcame her skepticism and she was soon filling in the gaps I hadn't been able to. She ran his name with the Department of Justice and came up with a four-page criminal record going back to when he was still a kid. I had a copy of it in my coat pocket. That, and notes from a couple of interviews with other men who had allowed themselves to be seduced by him, to their ultimate detriment. As for

McBeth, she was, at this very moment, at the rented house in the valley where Sam Bligh was filming his latest porn opus. The circle was closing.

"You make good coffee," I said.

He frowned; he knew I was being patronizing and didn't like it.

"You seemed surprised when I called you on the phone," I continued.

"I didn't know what you wanted," he replied.

"Do you now?"

"I think so," he said, his eyes steady on mine. He wore a white shirt, the top three buttons undone to reveal smooth flesh. I'd never been alone with him before. He was a different person alone than he was with Bligh, compared to whom he seemed comic relief. But alone, the contrast between the young body and old face was erotic rather than comic, conveying both innocence and availability. Nor was it crudely done; he was someone with considerable experience of being desired.

"When is Sam due back?" I asked him.

He smiled at me. "We have time."

"Does he mind this, your seeing other guys?"

"I'm particular," he replied.

"Oh, how's that?"

He stretched, the slender body tilting forward for my benefit. "I'm choosy. Sam takes good care of me, but I don't want to depend on him for everything."

"I understand," I said. "God bless the child that's got his own, right?"

His eyes narrowed suspiciously. "What does that mean?"

"It's an old Billie Holiday song," I told him. "It means we all have to watch out for ourselves."

"Exactly."

"So, what do we do now, Tommy?"

He got up, kicked off his shoes, pulled his shirt over his head and peeled off his jeans and said, "You'll think of something."

"I just have one question."

"What's that?"

"Did you really think you'd get away with murdering Chris Chandler?"

His face went blank. He pulled away from me and groped for his pants. "I don't know what you're talking about," he said, as he stuffed himself into them. "But you better get out of here before Sam comes back."

"We have time," I reminded him.

"What do you want?"

"I want to tell you a story," I said, "and I want you to tell me how it ends. Sit down."

He hesitated, calculating the situation, then smiled at me and said, "You must be crazy. If you don't leave, I'll have to call the cops."

"Don't worry about the cops," I said. "They'll be along. Now sit down."

He sat.

"So this is my story, Tommy. There was a kid from a pretty good family who had a mean streak in him. He spent most of his teenage years in and out of juvenile hall for petty stuff, at first, but gradually it escalated and he ended up doing some serious time because it seems he killed someone, an older man who the boy said had tried to sexually molest him. Are you with me, so far?"

He watched me without expression, as untroubled as if we were discussing the weather. I didn't think it was a put-on; as far as he was concerned, we could have been discussing the weather.

"That was a clever defense," I continued, "what with everyone concerned about child molesters, but the victim had some good friends who came into court and said, yes, he had a sexual relationship with the boy, but it was consensual."

"They lied," he said. "He hurt me."

"The judge didn't buy it," I said. "He convicted the boy of second-degree murder and shipped him off to youth camp for a couple of years. Then the boy was released and the juvenile court record sealed to protect the boy from having this unfortunate incident follow him around for the rest of his life."

"This is really boring," he said.

"It gets better," I said. "The boy was released and managed to stay out of trouble for a while. Legal trouble, anyway. He did have a lot of problems with his parents and they finally threw him out. The boy knocked around and ended up in Hollywood where he was picked up a couple of times for prostitution and once for an assault on one of his tricks. It was a pretty serious assault, but the trick decided against testifying because he wanted to avoid the publicity. I think, though I can't prove it, that the boy beat up some of his other customers, too, but they were too afraid even to press charges. Am I right?"

"I never hurt anyone," he said.

I watched the flicker of muscle beneath the skin; his body was like tensile steel.

"Not in a fair fight, maybe," I said, "but some half-drunk, beer-bellied closet case wouldn't have been any match for—this boy. Anyway, he learned a valuable lesson on the street. He learned that men with secrets are easy targets for all kinds of intimidation. Eventually, it occurred to him that maybe there was more to be gained here than the pleasure of beating someone senseless. Maybe there was money to be made. At any rate, he was tired of the streets. So, when the old guy in a wheelchair approached him about being in the movies, he went for it."

"I never made a video," he said, angrily.

"No, the boy saw there was not much future in that, so he concentrated on making himself invaluable to the old man who'd taken him in. And, as luck would have it, the old man needed an assistant just then. Since the old man was in a risky kind of business, he made a point of entertaining powerful, closeted men who could protect him from police harassment, and one of the services he provided to these powerful, closeted men was the occasional companion. So, from time to time, our boy was expected to bed one of these guys. Being an observant kind of boy, he soon noticed that many of these men, despite their power, were as scared of being found out as the tricks who used to pick him up on Santa Monica Boulevard."

Tommy picked up his shirt from the floor and made a show of putting it on.

"Be patient," I told him. "I'm almost through. The point is that the boy figured out he could blackmail some of these men. So that's what he did, behind the old man's back, of course. After all, the old man was doing a little blackmailing of his own and he wouldn't have appreciated the double-dipping. The boy was careful who he put the squeeze on. He chose married men. Well off, but not so rich they could afford to lose their jobs in a scandal. Men with the kind of jobs that kept them in the public eye. Say, an anchorman for a local TV news show. Or the pastor of a big church in the South Bay."

He opened his mouth to speak, but thought better of it.

"Surprised, Tommy?" I asked. "You shouldn't be. Most people get sick of being blackmailed eventually. You know that. Take this judge. He came to a couple of Sam's parties and he had victim written all over him. Our boy made his move, put on a private show for him, maybe, like the one you put on for me earlier. That would've been hard to resist. You're good."

"Let me show you how good I am."

"I haven't finished my story. The boy put on his show and the judge fell for him. They carried on for a while and then the boy began to hit him up for money. The judge paid. He couldn't risk exposure, not with a wife and a family and his respectable career on the line. But it sobered him up. He realized that as long as he continued to lead a double life, he would also be prey to the scum."

His eyes darkened in anger. "Who was the scum when my dick was in his mouth and his wife was sitting at home with the kid?"

"You are a sensitive boy," I said. "I had no idea."

"Fuck you, faggot."

"I detect a little confusion here, but let me continue. The point is, our boy unwittingly began to push the judge out of the closet, and then the judge met another boy. A good kid, basically. The judge fell in love with him and he left his wife to try to make a better life for himself, one where he didn't have to lie about who he was. But even then, he still allowed himself to be blackmailed. For years, he'd lived in fear of what would happen to his marriage if his wife discovered he was gay, and now he was afraid of what his lover would do if he found out about our boy and the blackmail. Fear is a hard habit to break."

Tommy laughed, a sharp, mocking laugh. "You don't get it," he said. "He wasn't afraid. He was still fucking me."

"Not after he met Zack," I said.

He laughed again and mimicked, " 'Not after he met Zack.' You don't know anything. He didn't want Zack. He wanted me. He was fucking me right up to—" He bit off the end of the sentence. "He needed to feel guilty about something. It got him off, coming here when Zack was at work and screwing me. He couldn't get it up without someone to cheat on."

"I don't believe you," I said. "He hadn't exchanged one kind of closet for another. You went to see him the night he was killed. He told you he didn't want to see you again. He told you he wasn't going to give you another cent. He told you he was going to tell Zack everything. You couldn't take it, so you reverted to your old habits and killed him. Then you heard someone coming down the hall and hid in the bathroom. It was Zack. After he left, you took the weapon and brought it here. When Zack came to see Bligh in a panic, you saw your chance and planted the weapon in Zack's apartment, then called the cops and told them they could find it there. Bligh sent Zack up to his cabin and you called the cops again and told them he was hiding there. Those calls were recorded," I lied. "It won't be hard to prove it's you on the tape."

He made a dive for the door. I let him go. He wouldn't get far, not with the cops waiting at the gate.

A couple of hours later, I was sitting in the courtyard of a coffeehouse on Santa Monica Boulevard. Above the murmur of a fountain, Louis Armstrong sang "Lush Life" over outdoor speakers. McBeth made her way across the cobblestones balancing cups of coffee in her hands. She set them down on the table, pulled out a metal chair and sat down, reaching for a cigarette from the pack in the pocket. Her blazer fell open, revealing her gun. She tugged the coat closed.

Lighting up, she said, continuing our earlier conversation, "You didn't exactly get him to confess."

"I know," I said. "But when he told me Chris was still seeing him even after he met Zack, it caught me off guard, so I threw everything I had at him. He did try to run," I pointed out. "That shows consciousness of guilt."

"It's a circumstantial case at best," she replied, flicking ash from her lapel. "We can't even put him at the scene."

"He was at the restaurant where Zack worked the night Chris was killed," I reminded her. "But he lied about eating dinner there. Zack said he talked to him in the bar at the beginning of his shift and mentioned that Chris was at the courthouse, but then he left."

She shrugged. "Circumstantial."

"He had access to the key to Zack's apartment while Zack was at Bligh's."

"I know all that," she replied, irritably. "But no one saw him there."

We drank coffee in silence. "What about Bligh?" I asked. "Did he say anything useful?"

She shook her head. "Bligh won't talk. He doesn't want to incriminate himself."

"We've still got the anchorman and the priest."

"Yeah, but all they can give us is his m.o."

"Well, the D.A.'s just going to have to go with what he's got," I said.

"Yeah," she replied, glumly. "On the bright side, you guessed right about him. That was nice work."

"Thanks," I said, "but I wasn't entirely right. I didn't figure that Chris was still having sex with him after he met Zack."

"That really bothers you, doesn't it?"

I nodded. "I guess Chris wasn't as far out of the closet as I thought he was."

"From what I understand," she said, "it's a pretty deep place."

27

TWO WEEKS PASSED. TOMMY WAS ARRAIGNED ON CHARGES OF first-degree murder. Privately, McBeth told me that the D.A. was already talking about pleading it down to second degree or even voluntary manslaughter because, based on the evidence, if the case went to trial there was no more than a fifty-fifty chance of a conviction of any kind. I shared her pessimistic assessment, but there wasn't anything I could do about it.

Zack called and I had to break the news to him of Chris's infidelity, if that's the word for it. He was as upset by it as Bay had been when Chris left her for him. I couldn't find it in myself to defend Chris to him as I had with Bay. Chris, it seems, had been a lot more troubled and self-destructive than I'd ever realized. Maybe none of us had known him after all.

At any rate, I didn't have much time to spare for Chris Chandler. Josh had been almost a month off all his drugs and he was so weak that he now seldom got out of bed. He was lucid when he was awake, but he slept most of the time, and there was little I could do but sit with him and wait for the end. After all the dramatic ups and downs of the past couple of years, the quiet with which he was dying seemed almost anticlimactic. The house was as hushed as a hospital zone, with nurses around the clock, his parents and sisters coming and going, and Singh dropping by at least once a day. None of us had much to say to each other. Not that there was any animosity between his family and me, not even with his father; it was the waiting that exhausted us.

I was sitting in the bedroom one afternoon reading Dickens to him while he slept the dazed, light sleep into which he slipped more and more often, when I heard the doorbell ring. The day nurse, a motherly gay black man named Robin, came in and told me, "There's a lady who wants to talk to you, Henry."

I put the book down and asked, "Did she give you her name?"

"Bay," he said.

"Okay, thanks," I said, getting up. "You mind reading to him?"

Robin picked up the book. *"Bleak House,"* he read. "Sounds depressing."

"It's not," I said. "He says it's his favorite novel because it has lawyers and a happy ending. I'll be back in a few minutes."

Bay was standing at the window doors looking out at the canyon. She was in slacks and a pink sweater. She turned when she heard me enter the room and smiled wanly.

"I hope this isn't a bad time," she said.

"No, it's fine," I replied. "It's good to see you, Bay. Can I get you something to drink?"

"No, thanks, I can't stay. Mind if I sit?"

"Please."

We sat across from each other. "The man who answered the door was a nurse," she said.

"Yeah," I said.

"Josh?" she ventured.

I nodded. "He's dying."

"I'm so sorry, Henry."

"I appreciate that," I said. She looked at a loss for words, so I added, "It's all right, Bay. There's nothing anyone can do now."

"I'll pray for him," she said.

I let a moment pass, then said, "Did I tell you it's good to see you?"

"Yes, it's good to see you, too, Henry. I guess the last time we talked wasn't so pleasant for either of us."

"You had a right to be mad at me," I said. "I lied to you."

She shook her head. "Chris lied to me," she replied. "You just got caught in the middle. In your situation, I probably would've done the same thing. It wasn't about you, it was about Chris."

"Chris was a troubled guy," I said.

She released a low laugh. "That's an understatement. But you know what happens in a marriage is that you get so used to the other person you stop seeing him as someone separate. You just assume he wants what you want and thinks the way you think. You forget he might have his own—what? Desires? Longings? Secrets?" She tilted her head and regarded me quizzically. "Do you know what I mean?"

I thought of the morning Josh told me he was in love with another man, and said, "I know exactly what you mean. We never know anyone as well as we think we do."

"No, never. That's why I didn't come sooner, to tell you about Joey."

"Joey?" I said. "What about him?"

"You thought he killed Chris," she said. "So did I."

I stared at her.

"You see," she continued, "after Chris left me, I wasn't sure I knew anyone anymore, not even myself, so when Joey told me he'd found his father's body that night, I didn't know what to think."

"What happened?"

She said, "He had dinner with Chris that night. They had a big fight and Joey ran out on him. Later, he went to the court, to apologize, he says, though I think it was probably to pick another fight with him. He says when he got there Chris was already dead. He got scared and left. He went to his grandfather and told him what had happened. Dad told him to keep his mouth shut, but, unlike Chris, Joey's never been any good at keeping secrets from me and I suspected the worst. Mind you, I couldn't bring myself to ask him point blank if he'd killed Chris, I just assumed it."

"Did your father also suspect him?"

"Not until you talked to him. That really shook him up. I went to that hearing to try to make some kind of deal with you, but I lost my nerve. When Detective McBeth lied on the stand, I saw my chance to help you, indirectly, by telling the prosecutor I'd given McBeth Chris's keys. I thought if I helped you get Zack Bowen off, you'd forget about Joey."

"You didn't think Zack killed Chris."

She shrugged. "I didn't know, because I didn't know if Joey was telling me the truth about what happened that night. I went over it again and again and I just couldn't say for sure."

"What do you think now?"

"This man they've arrested. He killed Chris."

"Tommy Callen. I think so, too, but the evidence isn't all that compelling."

"Joey saw him that night," she said.

"What?" I said incredulously.

"He was on the news the other night," she said. "Joey told me he saw him in the parking lot just before he went up to see his father. He's sure of it."

"What exactly did he see?"

"He saw this man get into a car and drive out of the lot. He remembers because the man left in a hurry."

"Does Joey remember whether the weapon that was used to kill Chris was still in his chambers when he went up there?"

"I don't know," she said. "I didn't ask him."

"Is he sure enough about seeing Tommy to testify?"

"Yes," she said. "Dad doesn't want him to, but I told him he owed it to Chris."

"Why is your father opposed?"

"Dad thinks Chris did enough damage to the family," she said. "Chris betrayed him, too, you know. He loved him like a son."

"I remember," I said.

"I want this man in prison," she said. "He deserves it. I don't care if we have to air some dirty linen to do it."

"Then you need to go to the police," I said.

She nodded. "I know. But I wanted to tell you first, so we could be friends again, if that's possible."

"I hope so," I said.

She got up, "I better go. I'm sure you want to get back to Josh, but Henry, there's one more thing I have to tell you."

"What is it, Bay?"

"The thing that got Joey so mad at his father that night, the reason I thought he might have killed him."

Puzzled, I said, "You mean other than the fact that he'd left you?"

She nodded. "That wasn't it. I mean, Joey was furious at Chris for that, but he wouldn't have killed him because of it. It was the other thing."

"What other thing?"

"He told Joey he was HIV-positive," she said.

"Oh, God."

"You need to tell his friend Zack to get tested," she said.

"What about you?"

"I've already been tested," she said, slowly. "I'm positive."

In the Gospel of Thomas, Jesus says, "If you bring forth what is within you, what you bring forth will save you. If you do not bring forth what is within you, what you do not bring forth will destroy you." I'd run across that text when I was an undergraduate, still struggling with my own sexual nature, and it had spoken so chillingly and directly to me that I'd written it down on a scrap of paper and carried it in my wallet. The paper was long gone, but the words were imprinted in my memory and they came to me now, as I sat in the living room after Bay had gone, thinking about Chris Chandler, who had waited too long to bring forth that which was within him. When he did, he'd left a trail of destruction in his wake that would continue long after his murder at the hands of the sociopath. I was all wrong about Chris Chandler. He hadn't come out of the closet in a surge of midlife decisiveness. He'd been driven out by guilt over what he'd done to Bay and his inability to tell her. Chris had simply moved from one room of his closet to another until nothing could reach him, not even love, and his closet had become his coffin.

I would have to tell Zack. The thought of it made me sick at heart. I could only hope he'd been safe with Chris, a chance Bay never had since she knew nothing of Chris's other life. I could have told her. The thought made me even sicker. Had Bay intended that? The layers of deceit among the three of us were so thick I no longer knew what to think of the Chandlers. I would work my way through that maze another time. For now, I needed the simplicity of Josh and me. I got up and went back into the bedroom where Robin was standing beside the bed, peering into Josh's eyes, *Bleak House* abandoned on the floor.

"What's wrong?" I demanded.

"I think he's in a coma," Robin said. "You sit with him. I'll call Dr. Singh."

He hustled out of the room. I sat down at the edge of the bed and stared into Josh's motionless eyes. Only the faint stream of his breath indicated there was any life left in him. I clutched at his hand.

"Josh," I said, brokenly.

I felt, or imagined I felt, a slight compression of his hand in mine. And then he was gone.